'ine Lion's
Courtship

by
Annelie Wendeberg

Books by this author:

Mickaela Capra Series:
1/2986
fog

Anna Kronberg Series
The Devil's Grin
The Fall
The Journey
Moriarty
The Lion's Courtship

Find out more at:
www.anneliewendeberg.com

Bullet Hole

The soul is always beautiful.

Walt Whitman

April 1885

The thief's fingers slip over his lockpicks. Blood congeals at once, warm mud on gritty cast iron. The alley is as dark as a dog's innards, for gas has been short this week.

His fingertips probe the keyhole once more, then he chooses a lockpick of a different shape. He feels himself weaken by the moment. Knees now trembling, his tongue so parched that his throat doesn't permit a swallow. Blood loss is buzzing in his ears and the makeshift bandage cuts into his thigh, but fails to staunch the flow.

His last hope is on the other side of this goddamned door.

He presses his brow against the cracked wood. A cuss rolls up his throat. He calms his trembling hands and lets his tools sink back into the lock. Two clicks. His heart leaps.

***

Her ears pick up a noise. Shock propels her out of bed before her legs are fully awake. Someone is climbing the stairs. Someone large; someone who doesn't sound like the drunkard of a landlord. And yet — could it be an overdose of gin that makes his stomps so weak and unsteady?

She wraps a robe around her nightgown and snatches a knife from the kitchen, her knuckles rock-hard from the tightness of her grip. She lights a candle and — with her heart pounding against her ribs — she presses a bare heel up against the door. As though she could block an intruder.

A fist hits wood. Twice.

'Who's there?'

''Ave been shot,' a stranger grunts.

She moves her foot a little and cracks the door open, peeking out with one eye. Dim light pours through the narrow gap. At first, her gaze falls on his chest where the head of a person her size would have been, then travels farther up. Fear creeps in with each additional inch. There is blood on his forehead and temples — streaks from wiping away sweat. A shock of orange hair, eyes pale blue, his face ashen.

For reassurance, she grabs her knife tighter and presses its handle against her spine. The blade is long enough to be driven through a grown man's chest, into his heart and lungs. Even a man that massive.

'Pal o' mine told me yer a nurse.' His voice is a harsh groan. He blinks and sways, about to fall through the door.

Reflex-like, she steps aside and admits him. *Heavy blood loss, shock.* Her mind repeats her diagnosis while calculating the risk of getting hurt tonight.

She points him to a chair, reconsiders, then pulls it up to him. The door frame creaks as he holds onto it. He topples into the room and sits down with a huff. She slips the knife through the belt of her robe, reminding herself to keep her front facing the man at all times.

Blood leaks onto the floorboards. His right boot left dark prints. Thick droplets trail from door to chair.

'Lean back,' she commands, reaching toward him. Shame wipes away his paleness when she helps him get his trousers off. She tugs at them, huffs and shouts, 'Lift your hindquarters, man!' and yanks them down. They get stuck on his heels. A final tug and the bloody things fly out of sight, together with his boots. Sharp scissors slice off the drenched leg of his drawers, the cold metal barely touching his skin. She fetches a tourniquet from her doctor's bag and strangles his thigh.

His trembling is about to tip him off the chair.

'Bloody Christ!' he groans as she pours a burning liquid over the wound.

'Clean shot,' she notes. 'Went straight through. Major blood vessels seem to be intact.' The pair of long pliers she holds in her hand are chucked back into the bag. His panicked expression disappears with them.

She takes a roll of bandages and wraps them around his trembling thigh. 'Can you stand up?' she asks.

He makes a face like a puppy about to be drowned. His eyes begin to roll, lids flutter. His head tips, then his shoulders.

She slaps his cheek. Once, twice. The sharp pain pulls him upright. She tugs at his arm and barks an order he doesn't seem to understand, but he regains his senses, enough to stand on one leg, yet not enough to prevent him from slumping on her shoulder. They toddle a few steps. Then her mattress hits him in the face.

'Holy show!' he mutters and shuts his eyes.

***

His face is caressed by a soft pillow. The thief inhales the scent of freshly laundered linen, his breath sighing through his nostrils. As he turns his head, his stubble scrapes along the cotton. A down pillow? He never...

His eyes snap open. A cockroach is perched on a chair in front of him. 'And who are you?' he spits.

'Barry,' the little dirt bag answers with a grin, showing his four missing front teeth. His hands and face are of a greyish-brown hue from underuse of soap and water. His attire is a mosaic of patches. Only the knife — with a blade the length of his shin — is an uncommon feature for a street urchin.

The thief blinks. His brain feels a little sluggish. When he moves his legs, a jab of pain reminds him of the previous night. A woman had plugged a gunshot wound close to his privates. He had almost puked on her floor. Or had he? A quick glance tells him the room is clean. Unusually clean. 'Did you butcher the nurse with that thing?' He gestures at the knife.

Barry rolls his eyes and squeaks, 'She asked me to keep an eye on you.'

The boy is only six years old. At least that's what he believes. He couldn't tell what day or year it is, but he knows precisely that the thief could snap his neck without effort. To demonstrate the fearsomeness of his weapon and the fearlessness of himself, he taps the knife's tip against his fingernails and extracts minuscule dirt sausages from underneath each one of them.

'Why would she say that?' the thief asks.

'None of your business.' The harsh dismissal sounds funny, coming from such a young throat.

The man pushes himself up and all blood drains from his face. Grunting, he makes it to the edge of the bed and plops both feet down on the floor.

Barry points his knife to the far side of the room. 'She said you can go home if you make it all the way to your trousers without *fainting*.' He speaks the last word as though he is a fine lady, or, at least, in an attempt to sound like one. Not that he ever saw a fine lady, or ever heard one speak, let alone has the ability to identify one should she cross his path, which — in itself — is quite impossible.

Squinting, the thief assesses the distance. His trousers are draped over a chair, the backrest peeks through the bullet hole. The blood is gone. She must have cleaned them last night. What an odd woman. His eyes search the floorboards again to make sure he had indeed not puked in this impeccable room. He can't even find signs of his blood, let alone prints of his dirty boots.

He shrugs, pushes off the bed, and staggers forward. 'Bloody Christ!' he huffs and steadies himself on the wall. The room spins a little. He walks carefully, scraping one of his square palms along the cracking plaster.

At last he reaches the chair and can lower his buttocks. The wood gives a pitiful screech. With much effort, he inserts his throbbing leg into the trousers. The thick dressing hampers the progress. Sweat begins to itch on his forehead.

'You look green,' quips the boy.

The thief breathes heavily, buttons his fly, and stands up. 'I will take that chair with me,' he says.

Barry's eyebrows go up, all the way until they are hiding underneath his cloth cap. He shakes his head and lifts the knife as a reminder.

'I need it as a crutch. I'll return it.'

The boy's head is still wagging.

The man gets angry. His leg is aching badly and he isn't sure how long he can remain upright.

The boy points with his knife. *Bloody Christ*, the thief thinks when he spots a makeshift crutch right next to the nurse's bed. The usual variety of cuss words seems to fail him today. He touches his head to make sure he hasn't been shot there, too.

Out on the street, the man's stomach growls. He is so hungry, he could eat an entire cow, all with tail and horns and feet. A few pies will have to do, though. His tongue asks for a pint of ale, but his mind calculates the budget. Home-brewed tea it must be instead. That disastrous burglary last night has left him with nothing but a shilling, a hole in his thigh, and a rent needing to be paid.

Huffing, he leans against a wall when he remembers his lockpicks. They are still at the nurse's place. Too exhausted to hunt for food, he pushes towards his quarters — a small room in a run-down house. Yet, not as decrepit as most of the neighbouring buildings.

The familiar creak of his door, the smell of cold tallow candle, his bed in the far corner — all irresistibly inviting to shed his tiredness with a good long sleep. But first, he needs to quench his thirst and, in three large gulps, he drains all the water left in the jug. With a slice of stale bread in his hand, he shuffles to his sleeping corner. The straw crackles as his healthy knee hits the mattress. He pulls in the injured leg, curls up, chews on the crust, and begins to snore not two minutes later.

A shot jerks him awake. Or was it a bang at the door? There, another one. 'Who is it?' he grumbles loud enough to be heard through the thin wood.

'It is I,' she answers.

He tries to recall her name. Had she not given it, last night? He struggles to get up, glad he's still dressed, and hobbles to the door.

'You forgot your lockpicks.'

Her short hair shocks him. Her black curls, tucked behind both ears, can barely hold on to that delicate ledge. Did he not look at her last night, or could he simply not remember?

Her chest is almost bosom-less. With her high cheekbones and her nose and eyebrows as sharp as a bird of prey's, determination screams at him from every feature. He almost takes a step back. *She's barely half your size, goddammit!* he scolds himself.

When she walks past him, his gaze follows her. Her shoulder blades move beneath the soft fabric of her dress and he thinks of folded wings too small for take-off.

With his tools still in her hand, she points to his leg. 'Surely Barry told you that I have to change the dressing once a day?'

Dumbstruck, he shakes his head. She slams her bag on his table and lifts an eyebrow.

Unspeaking, he shuts the door and walks to a chair. His leg is happy not to have to support his weight any longer.

'Take your trousers off.'

He coughs. His cheeks blush orange, almost reaching the shade of his hair as he fumbles on the buttons and awkwardly follows her order.

12

'You broke into my house,' she says while unwrapping the bandages.

'I'm Garret,' he mumbles.

She pokes a finger into the reddened flesh around his gunshot wound. He suppresses a wince.

'What the devil?' he shouts as she bends down, her nose about to touch his thigh.

'Smells clean. No infection. Good.' She straightens up, smiles, and the thief is ready to pass out. *She just had her face in my crotch!* his mind screams. *Almost.*

The woman takes a bottle and a kerchief from her bag, spreads brown liquid around the wound and gently dabs at it. Clear fluid seeps out the hole, mingling with the brown. The thief, now pale, tries hard to think of his grandmother; her last days, toothless, hairless, hallucinating, and pooping large round balls like a horse's. It doesn't help. He sees the woman's gaze flicker to the conspicuous bulge in his one-legged drawers when she dresses his wound.

She straightens up and smooths the front of her dress. Her jaws are working. With a voice as frigid as the sleet rapping against Garret's window, she says, 'If you don't wash with soap every day, your wound will get infected and you'll die. I cannot saw that leg off so close to the hip. Tomorrow, I'll show you how to change bandages and disinfect the wound. Have a good day.'

The door slams shut.

Garret sits on his chair, trembling and unsure whether he can get his trousers back up without fainting.

***

The woman steps out of the doorway, wiping dark memories away, and shaking off her paleness. 'Thank you for waiting, Barry,' she says and pulls the shawl farther up her neck. The boy nods, gifts her a smile, says, 'See ya, Anna,' and then dashes off.

She hurries in the opposite direction, three blocks down a road, crowded by people, their refuse, and hotchpotch.

She stops at a corner, takes a good look around to make sure no one followed her, and then sneaks into an alley to disappear at the back door of the cobbler's.

Burglary

The conifer pokes at Garret's neck. He moves the twig aside and changes position, careful to remain invisible. The jemmy, the glass knife, a wood cutter, and a length of rope, all wrapped in strips of cloth, press against his stomach. His lockpicks were made by his own hands and this is where he keeps them while his gaze attaches to a villa thirty yards in front of him. One mightily splendid house if he'd compare it with the one he lives in. But he doesn't. It would be a waste of time and energy. To him, this villa is not the home of someone. It's a strongbox he will pry open and gut.

Despite the late hour, light seeps through a pair of windows; all others are black holes in the ivy-covered stone walls. The gate had been locked just before dinner and the main entrance a few minutes past eleven o'clock when the servants were about to retire. A well-kept household, it appears, with the staff having finished their chores before midnight.

The two lit windows, Garret learned on his first night under the tree, belong to the bedroom of the lady of the house. Her husband, people say, took a bullet in his hindquarters during the Crimean War. There it remained, a few years, until his body gave in to recurring infections. The lover his wife had taken might or might not have sped up the husband's disintegration. But disintegrate he did and now rots six feet underground, mucky London soil covering his brow.

The considerably younger replacement visits daily, often arriving at supper time, to climb out of the bedroom window around three o'clock in the morning. This man is an entirely different kind of thief. One no accomplished cracksman like Garret wants to be compared with. That man had taken a mistress rich enough to pay for whatever he fancied until the end of her days. Every time Mr Lover smoothed his clothes — crumpled from his latest climbing adventure — he patted a bulge in his waistcoat pocket and strolled off with a satisfied grin.

Garret knows that whatever is hidden in the folds of finest wool and silk will be turned into money when the opportunity presents itself.

Stomach yowling and wound throbbing, he shifts his weight ever so gently. The church bell calls four in the morning and the widow's lover still hasn't exited the house. The bedroom is dimly lit, but no movements can be seen.

He toys with his thoughts and his lockpicks, turning them over, feeling them from one side, then the other. He could do it tomorrow. But his hunger and overdue rent urge him forward.

At least he can take a look. Go in through the front door and not through a cut-open window pane. If he leaves no traces and takes something inconspicuous — pieces of knick-knacks no one will miss but good enough to feed him for a few days — he can return and take the valuables later. His

16

stomach gives yet another painful grumble and his brain agrees.

With surprising speed and silence, the large man makes his way towards the main entrance. A moment later, he disappears in the shadows of the oak door's deep frame. His hand probes the lock, a sharp little hole with indentations and spikes. His fingertips caress it like a lover's, trying to tickle secrets from its depths. And yes, it accommodates his need and tells him which of his tools might fit. He tips his chin in acknowledgement, then tries one lockpick, then another, until he's rewarded with two soft clicks.

Gently, he pushes the door. It budges a fraction, then stops. He had expected the bolt. Garret chooses a slender metal sheet from his collection of tools and pushes it between the door and its frame. With dozens of small movements, he slides the bolt aside, then steps into the dark entrance hall and shuts the door behind him.

The silence from outside is replaced with muffled voices and dim light trickling down the stairwell. If not for the hunger, Garret would walk back out immediately.

No use in throwing a longing glance up the stairs. The jewellery will be in the lady's bedroom, very close and yet unreachable now.

He creeps through the hall into the first room to the right, strikes a match, looks around, then retreats. The drawing room contains nothing of interest to him.

He takes a door to the left. Same procedure. Lighting of a match, taking in all details, and etching the important ones into his mind before the flame can scorch his fingers. Darkness falls.

The voices are now just above him, muttering. The male voice defiant, the female voice accusing. Garret moves swiftly. He knows the distance to the objects of his desire, having seen them for a moment in the small bubble of light.

He snatches two tiny statues. A letter opener and a crystal ashtray find a new home in his coat pockets, too, and he is ready to leave. Just then, he hears a cry of 'No!'

Garret presses against the wall behind the brocade curtains. Hasty steps clatter down the stairs, then a second pair of feet follows. A female, 'Oh, my love, don't leave me!' quivering with despair. Both come to a halt, then move to meet at the middle of the stairs. A sigh and then another, before they make their way back up. Just as the bed begins to creak, Garret leaves his hiding spot.

Down at the street he chuckles, slapping his healthy thigh. 'Womenfolk!' he groans and begins strolling towards St Giles. At the back door to the duffer, he steps in without knocking.

'What've ya got?' the scrubby man enquires, barely tearing his eyes off a well-thumbed book, its binding greasy, pages dog-eared.

The man considers himself well read, although the reading of tuppence material with women in all kinds of positions, usually with at least

18

one man attached to their orifices, doesn't quite meet the classical definition of *reading* material.

The duffer remains sitting, not the least bothered by the Irishman's presence. If he were to rise all the way to the tip of his toes, his nose might reach Garret's shoulders.

'Only the best,' Garret says with false conviction, then holds out his square palms.

'I'll be damned if it ain't the ugliest fat little angels I've ever seen!' The man stares down at the two tiny statues, raises an eyebrow at Garret, and knows this man is desperate. 'Two pence each.'

They haggle until the thief's brow perspires. Angry, he leaves. A public house is precisely what he needs now, or that howling stomach of his will scare off everyone, including the rats that scamper across his path.

Three pies and two pints of ale later, an elbow — complete with buffed sleeve and a cloud of perfume — pokes his side.

'Oy, Thrulow,' Garret says, 'no gentlemen to flog today?'

Gloved hands flutter down upon his arm. Beneath her blue velvet dress, a corset shapes her body to a perfect hourglass. Thick blond curls pour from beneath the bonnet and course down her spine, cheekily pointing at her hindquarters. With her fine clothes, she almost looks like a lady, if not for that squeezed-up bosom. Birching some noble lord's backside while a *fricktrix* was busy at the man's front paid very well indeed.

She scowls at him. 'Took a day's vacation to see my mother.'

'I see,' says Garret, thinking that if she would abandon her *calling* for a single day only to see her mother, he would eat a broom handle.

'You look worn,' she purrs. 'Fancy some recreational activities?'

He feels himself grow hot. The frisky and merry-arsed Thrulow makes his privates whimper. Not that he feels drawn to that bloody flogging business, but this woman's backside surely had magnetic qualities.

'I have no money,' he replies. 'Besides, I prefer to remain in one piece.' *And you are too expensive,* he adds silently.

She pokes him again. This time harder. 'You could do me, if you like.'

'Thrulow, I have no money and I don't like your birches, nettles, and whatnot. If I want to hit someone, I pick a fella my size. Never beat a woman and never will.'

'Whatever you wish, my dear.' The sugary lilt of her voice goes unnoticed by him. Her hand on his arm doesn't, though. Heat spreads from there down to his balls. She moves closer to him until he feels her bosom press against his shoulder.

'Good night, then, Garret,' she breathes, mouth puckering, eyelashes waving. She turns around and swings her buttocks more than necessary when she walks out the door.

Garret presses his forehead against the wooden table top and counts to ten, thinking of the last time he'd paid a woman.

His encounters with the weaker sex are usually awkward and rather hasty. Bawdy women willingly lifted their skirts, as long as a shilling or two were involved, a dark alley could be found, and only the rats watched the rubbing, the grunting, the spending, and wiping off fluids. Often they said one thing and meant another, behaving as though they didn't want to have a man, as though they were well-bred and hard to get, all the while teasing him to come over and show them his manhood. Why some of his friends got married was a mystery to him.

His heart begins to flutter — an alarmingly unfamiliar condition — as the nurse's face shows up in his mind, her mouth slapping a command at him: *Take off your trousers!*

How come he doesn't even know her name?

Birth

Barry squats on the pavement. Often, he arrives much too early, like today, but the waiting doesn't bother him. He keeps forgetting which days are the Tuesdays and the Fridays, but he does take his part-time occupation seriously. He calls them "pie man nights," but only secretly, because the two are not going out to eat. They *work*.

People here think she's adopted him. But they have it all wrong. It was precisely the other way around. When Anna arrived in St Giles (Barry believes it to be long ago, but it's barely three months), she stood out like a peacock with her clean and well-kept clothes (nothing fancy, mind you) and her funny English. That she must be in the possession of a few shillings (guineas, even?) any half-talented ragamuffin could extract from the folds of her skirts was clear from day one.

Barry had made a spontaneous attempt at pickpocketing, together with his gang of street arabs. Three of them bumped into her and toppled her over. Easy as crap. Barry probed her clothing with quick hands, and that was easy, too. But he couldn't find anything. Not even a handkerchief. Quite outraged, he had demanded where that lazy devil of a bludger was. At that, Anna calmly answered, 'Well, no hole in the head for me today, I guess.'

Barry can remember this one sentence more clearly than most things that have happened in his short life. He can still feel the wind in his gaping mouth. How odd that a woman like her knew what a bludger is — the strongest boy in a gang of arabs responsible to beat victims unconscious. Despite that bit of highly unusual education, Barry was convinced she is a lunatic when she — still lying on the pavement — informed them in a strange sing-song dialect that she is a nurse and will give free medical treatment to anyone in need.

He began revising his opinion two seconds later, theorising there might be at least some sense in her head when she said she would have to move to East End if she were to be mugged every time she crossed a street in St Giles. Besides, she stated solemnly, a nurse's income is rather meagre.

Some crank in Barry's head must have turned a wrong way, then, because he blurted, 'My mother used ter be a toffer,' as though that would relate to the topic in any way. He refrained from slapping his forehead, because that would have given him away.

'What's a toffer?' asked Anna as she stood and knocked the dirt off her skirt.

'A toffer is a posh trooper,' one of the other boys explained, eyebrows raised all the way to the brim of his cap, head bobbing. 'Now she's only a trooper. Old hag that.'

Deeply insulted, Barry had punched the boy's stomach and received a whack in his face in return. Blood spurted from cracked lips, and Anna had her first patient in St Giles.

Later, Barry explained to her that a trooper is a prostitute of the most wretched kind. The mixture of love and shame in his face had touched Anna's heart. She liked him at once.

***

For a while now, the two have been taking their nightly strolls together; the boy chattering away, the woman listening and her eyes sweeping the alleys. Often, all she can do is diagnose: syphilis, gonorrhoea, typhoid fever, consumption. With no miracle cure available, she suggests alleviation through rest, good food, and plenty of clean water, but none of those exist in the slums.

Rest means days without income. Clean water means to either walk very far, or to boil it using the scant wood, cardboard, or — for the comparatively well-to-do — coal. Good food means expenses beyond the affordable. She knows all this, but has learned that saying something is better than saying nothing at all.

She performs simple surgeries, sometimes amputations. She helps reluctant children out of their mothers' wombs, cleans and stitches up cuts. When, in a few months, the summer comes and heats up people's heads and makes them go wild about trifles, her supply of bandages, disinfectant, and opium will melt away in but a few days.

Tonight, Barry tells her everything he knows about skinners. Listening to his tales about women who lure children into alleys, strip them, and leave their victims to terror and nakedness while selling all their clothes, Anna strolls across Castle Street and watches how the evening sun dips the slums into a warm red, transforming tired faces into friendly ones.

Costermongers' barrows rattle past, their wares sold, the men worn but satisfied. Prostitutes step down onto the streets, shake out their skirts, and show their ankles. The cheeky ones among them even flash their stockinged knees, resulting in whistles from passers-by with too limited a budget. The ones who can afford the offered services curtly approach and mutter something only the woman can understand. An agreement is struck and the temporary couple enters the boarding house. Now, the hour is too early and the clientele too sober for anything cheap and hasty performed in the open.

Barry drifts towards their first mandatory stop — the penny pie man. Next to him sits his wife, her bare breast nourishing a youngster. A slender pipe is clamped between her teeth, producing an abundance of clouds and stink.

While Barry's chronically empty stomach is being filled with eel pie and he must cease his chatter for once, Anna gets a moment to think her own thoughts.

Talking while eating would result in loss of food through crumb expulsion — an unacceptable waste, according to the boy. Tonight, however, he breaks his rule. He elbows Anna's side, mumbles something that sounds like, 'Don't turn around,' and pulls her into an alley. 'That thief,' he whispers and sticks his nose around the corner, 'has been following us since... Oy! He's coming!' He snatches her hand and off they run. Through the alley, around a corner, through a partially unhinged back door, then along what looks like a corridor and out onto a street.

A woman calls to them from the other side, pointing to the house behind her. 'Will ya see tha' girl? She's makin' a ruckus since yesterday. Can't stand 'nother night like tha'!'

Barry makes round eyes, plucks at Anna's skirt, and shakes his head. Anna shrugs, lights her lantern, and enters, pulling the boy along.

A scream leaks down the dark stairwell. The rotten wood cries out with each step they take. Rats scamper up and down, untroubled by the newcomers and the shine of their oil lamp.

Following the noise, they step into a room. The setting sun doesn't reach through the windows. Anna cannot see whether they have been nailed shut or simply blocked with rubbish.

'Bedroom,' mumbles the boy sarcastically. They step over mouldy straw, potato bags, and piles of rags; neither of them feeling the urge to find out what's moving underneath. Someone lies curled up on the floor and pants, but onlookers block the view partially.

'Get them out of here,' Anna whispers to Barry. 'Then come back.' She squeezes through the

26

crowd and squats down, placing the lantern at her feet. 'I'm Anna. I'm a nurse. I can help you if you wish.' Her hand reaches out; the clean, white skin is in stark contrast to the grime on the girl's rags. Tears and dirt smudge her cheeks. A moan parts her lips, canker cracks, and yellow teeth gleam in the unsteady light.

The moan transforms into a shriek. While she waits for the contraction to subside, Anna takes in the room. Judging from the refuse, the number of makeshift mattresses, and the stink, more than twenty people must be sleeping here. Barry is trying to usher them out. His success rate amounts to about fifty per cent.

The girl regains her senses. 'Hello,' Anna says. 'Can I see how you and your child are doing?'

She nods and wipes spittle off her chin. Anna holds the lantern higher, illuminating the too-young face. 'Can I touch your stomach?'

'Already said yes, didn't I?' the girl hisses with the next contraction rolling over her.

Anna turns to see where Barry is, but the dark room has swallowed him. The hairs on her neck prickle. She feels a tension in the air, as though the walls are anticipating a thunderclap.

She collects more straw and a threadbare blanket, and spreads them out to make a softer bed. As the girl's contraction subsides, she helps her over and examines her abdomen. The child's head is already very low in the girl's pelvis. Her skirts aren't wet, the water bag must still be intact. 'How long have you been in labour?'

27

'Mighta been yesterday.'

'Your first child?'

'Na.' She waves her hand dismissively. 'First one died within the hour.'

Anna swallows a sigh. The girl couldn't be older than — what? Fifteen, sixteen years? Had she ever had a menstruation, going from childhood to first pregnancy to the second?

A tap on her shoulder makes her jump.

'Howshhe?' The voice of gin — raspy and about to tilt. It makes Anna feel alone and small. 'Vomman, anshwer mee!'

The girl in front of her begins to labour again, tearing her attention from the man behind her. A second later, pain jerks her upwards, together with a fist in her hair. 'Ashhked ya 'ow me girlie ish!' Spittle wets her cheek. The stink hauls bile up her throat. For a short moment, she considers using the jack-knife hidden in her sleeve, then decides against it. With all her might, she inserts her knee in the man's testicles. Grunting, he drops.

'What ya doin', ya trollop?' shouts the girl and kicks Anna's shin. The water breaks and gushes over her exposed legs. Her screams gain in pitch. People are moving closer now, mumbling demands Anna cannot understand over the girl's complaints. *Trapped*, is all she can think.

The crowd parts, and a man steps through. He dominates the room instantly. A skinny boy is peeking out from behind his legs. 'What ya doin' here?' Garret's voice booms.

'Knitting, quite obviously!'

28

The girl has just begun to push. 'Squat, if you can,' Anna suggests between two contractions.

The girl tries it once, but too exhausted to keep herself upright, she lies on her side again. Anna pushes the skirt farther up to watch the progress of the child through the birth canal. The head begins to crown. An inch forward, half an inch back; the rhythm of birth. Like waves, the contractions wash over the mother to carry the child ashore.

Anna cups her hands around the child's head as it descends. In the dim light of the lantern, the small face looks almost normal. Its blueish tint is so subtle that one might believe it's alive. But her fingers feel no pulse tapping against the slick skin of the child's throat. Once the shoulders are born, the boy slips out easily. A wrinkled corpse, so small it hurts Anna's heart. She picks him up and hands him to the girl. 'I'm sorry,' she whispers.

Neither of them speaks until the placenta wants to be born. 'Push once,' Anna says, tugging gently at the umbilical cord. A few moments later, Anna wipes her hands on a kerchief, checks the girl's bleeding, and rises to her feet.

The girl nods decisively and reaches out, offering the small corpse. Dumbstruck, Anna steps back. A large hand grabs her shoulder. 'Time to go,' Garret growls.

'You can sell it for a better price. At your hospital,' calls the girl and Anna pushes past Garret, past Barry, past the crowd, and stumbles down the stairs.

Heavy footfall sound behind her, a *clonk clonk* on cobblestones, then the call of a steam engine. 'Will ya stop, for Christ's sake!' She obeys and looks up at Garret, his hair wild, his arms hugging her doctor's bag.

'Where's Barry?' she asks.

'He's fine. Took 'im outa there an' sent 'im home. Shoulda given tha' boy a good spankin' for lettin' ya go into tha' house!' he barks.

She squints, as though his angry Irish accent would slide down easier that way.

'They're one o' the mad ones! Havin' four or five houses here with people like tha'! The fella ya knocked out? What did he do to ya?'

'He fucked the girl.'

'Well, congratulations!' He chucks her bag on the pavement, arms waving. ''E might 'ave, and all others migh' 'ave, too! Ya didn' hit *'em*. Want ter go back and make up for it?'

'Why did you follow me?'

'Ya went into tha' house, goddammit! Everyone 'ere knows they're mad. It's like an asylum for insane vermin. Only tha' the bars are missing and 'em inmates seek each other out. There is nothing in their heads, didn't ya see tha'? She wanted ya to sell her babe, knowing that ya get a better price for it and tha' ya won't keep the money for yerself!'

Anna nods, steps forward, and picks up her bag. 'Stop shouting at me. Stop throwing my medical instruments about, and most of all — stop believing I need your help,' she snarls and walks away.

After a few yards, she hears his footfalls yet again. 'Fancy a tea?' There's an apologetic tint in his voice.

She groans, her eyes search the tips of her boots for an appropriate answer. 'Brandy.'

He exhales in relief. 'Sounds good. I know a place. It's on me tonight,' he says as though they regularly went for a drink. He takes the bag from her hand and walks by her side.

'You know,' she begins, 'this is one of those nights I wish I lived in the countryside.'

'You are naive.'

'I know.'

'That life is tough. You get up before sunrise, work hard all day, go to bed late.'

'I know,' she says again, wondering how he could not know that *this* life is much harder.

'I grew up on a farm, a small sheep farm. My father taught me everything about it. How to care for the lambing ewes. How to move a herd, handle the dogs. When I was this tall,' Garret points to his knee, 'I helped my mother score and comb the wool. She always had soft hands...' he trails off.

Anna flicks her gaze to his large hands and tries to imagine them much smaller, the size of a boy's, helping a newborn lamb to reach its mother's teats.

'Here we are,' he says a minute later, opening the door of a public house for her. She reads "The Rat's Tail" scrawled in white paint over the door, then she's hit in the face by noise and tobacco smoke so thick one could move it with a shovel.

'Two brandies!' Garret slams a coin on the greasy wood.

He hands one glass to Anna. His eyes widen as she chucks it all down in one fluid move. 'Another one?'

'Hmm,' she agrees, tension slowly peeling off her. 'Do you have siblings?'

He turns away; his mouth sags. The word, 'Sister,' is barely audible. Garret's gaze sweeps the room. Suddenly, his bow crinkles and his eyes get stuck on something behind her back. She has no time to turn around. His fist flies past her face. A thud and a grunt behind her, then Garret shouts, 'Blasted cockchafer!' grabs her hand, and pushes past the clientele, parting the crowd like a large ship parts the ocean.

'What was that about?' she cries, once outside.

'Tha' fella... I know 'im. 'E was 'bout 'ter...' He looks down at her small hand in his large one. 'Never mind.'

She wiggles free and he's surprised by the twinge of disappointment this small gesture brings. 'Sorry for tha'... word.'

'Which one do you mean?' she barks. 'The blasted or the cockchafer?'

Garret's face reddens considerably. 'Never thought a woman like you would say that.'

'I *live* in St Giles,' she reminds him and walks ahead, tired and impatient with his brutishness.

'You grew up in the countryside?' he calls after her.

A smile scampers across her lips. He had listened. 'Yes.'

'Where?'

'In Germany.'

'Ha! And I thought you were Dutch.' He laughs. 'I knew a Dutch sailor once. Tattooed all over, that fella.' He gestures at his chest, his large arms thrashing like windmill blades. 'His ship got lost on its way down to India.'

Anna thinks of the Atlantic ocean, the waves rolling the vessel this way and that, the sunsets, and the vastness of the sea. She hums to herself.

'Have you seen the ocean?' he says. 'Oh, you must have!' He slaps his forehead. 'I meant the *real* ocean, not the channel.'

'No. Never,' she lies and turns away. 'It's late. I need to go home.'

He nods, surprised his chest would answer her dismissal with a painful clench. 'Oh!' says Garret. 'I don't even know your name.'

She laughs. 'I'm sorry, I thought I'd introduced myself weeks ago. Anna Kronberg.'

'Nice to meet you, Anna.'

'I'm a widow,' she lies.

On their silent way back, Garret decides that he'll keep an eye on this woman. Someone will take advantage of her someday, he is certain.

As they reach the door to her house, he stops and speaks to his hands. 'The fella in the pub was a pickpocket and a burglar. He tried to steal your money.'

'I noticed. I was about to tell him that I had nothing.'

'But we all know you're a nurse. You must earn at least fifty pounds a year.' He looks at her as though he is offended.

'And we all know,' she replies, 'that the nurse will leave if she doesn't feel safe here. And we all know that good pickpockets, burglars, or whores earn more than fifty pounds annually.' With that she turns and leaves him standing on the slick cobblestones.

Why, then, do you live here? Garret wonders. There is no reason for a non-criminal to seek refuge in a rookery.

Whores

As she turns into Clark's Mews, she cannot help but imagine the odour of rancid globs of ejaculate. Of course, one cannot smell it down here — not yet, not so close to the gutters and far from the moist sheets.

Girls and women between eleven and forty years of age litter the pavement. Their faces show anxiety, annoyance, or boredom. All customers were driven off by recent events. Income will be scarce for an hour or two, but once the winds have settled, men will return and quench their various appetites.

The only two men in sight belong here like the stink of semen and urine. Butcher and Nate, both providing a well measured dose of male brutishness to protect the flow of money to Clark's brothels — one known as "Mum's," the other as "Fat Annie's."

Anna is waved into Fat Annie's boarding house — decrepit, to say the least of it. The stairs yield under her weight as she climbs to the second floor; the wallpaper a pathetic joke with its leftovers slowly eaten by mould. Three tallow candles provide unsteady light. They must have been lit for her — an additional expense most of Fat Annie's girls aren't able to afford every day. But one of them was hurt tonight and now they act like a uniform mass of warrior ants against an intruder wasp.

Fingers point towards a room. Weeping trickles through the open door. She sheds all softness and steps in.

Blood on a wall. A thin sliver of dark red, arching from floor to ceiling. A blade must have been pulled through flesh with a violent swing.

A naked woman squats in the centre of the small room, held by two others. Whimpering seeps from all three mouths.

'What happened?' Anna kneels down in front of them. The two women peel off the third like petals of an opening flower. The girl's right cheek is parted by a hideous gash, mouth and wound are one. Rivulets crawl along her jawbone, drip from her chin down to breasts the size of small peaches. A scarlet band is parting around a pink nipple. The blood on her stomach is smudged by comforting hands; knees have cut through the congealing mess on the floor.

Anna places a hand on the trembling girl's arm. 'I will give you morphia for the pain and stitch up the wound. You will look like new.'

She shows no reaction. Her eyes are wide, pupils small like pinpricks, her skin ashen.

While the two women hold the third, Anna fastens the tourniquet and inserts a needle into the elbow bend. Eyelids flutter, taut muscles soften.

All three carry her to the bed — a greasy thing that smells of sweat and sperm about to ferment. Armed with iodine solution, needle, and thread, Anna begins to work.

'Do you know his name?' she enquires softly. Yielding to the pressure of the curved needle, the girl's skin breaks with a gentle pop, followed by the soft rasping of thread being pulled along.

'No,' one woman says. Palpable decisiveness in that lone word. 'She dinna want ter suck 'is cock,' she whispers, as though news of the neglect hadn't spread already. Bad for the business if you don't submit at first command.

'He was her first one,' explains the other.

Anna is closing the girl's wound with the most delicate stitches she can accomplish. Too disfigured, men will pay her too little or even avoid her altogether. She might starve to death. 'She will need help to heal,' she says.

One of them nods. Anna wonders whether she's the girl's friend, whether she can afford paying twice the food and rent. The thought is a wisp of naivety against the bland backdrop of life. One beat of lashes and hope vaporises.

She stands up and finds a woman leaning her massive backside against the door frame. 'I'll come back tomorrow night to examine the suture,' Anna says and gets a *shweeeet* of air sucked through fat lips as a reply. 'If she takes customers too early, this wound will never heal, and she'll be of no use to you.'

The madam tips her chin. Anna finds no pity in her face. A boy slips into the room, holding out a bowl with water. 'Ma'am,' he squeaks at Anna. She takes the offer and washes her hands. Brown lumps settle on the grey zinc bottom.

***

When she walks towards Clark's Mews' exit, passing Mum's boarding house, she hears laughter from within. A man steps out of the front door, burps, and tips his cloth cap at her.

She steers towards home, and tiredness settles heavily on her shoulders. Onlookers have long closed their windows, but have taken a minute to empty their chamberpots one last time before retiring for the night. Urine is still trickling down the walls and a fresh wave of sewage begins to crawl along the street. Anna wishes for rain and that her feet wouldn't feel so numb.

She crosses Broad Street onto Endell, passing dark shop windows and a group of what she believes are young thieves getting ready for the night. They greet her with a grin and a nod, hands deep in their trouser pockets. Otherwise, the streets are empty. Vendors will come back tomorrow around five in the morning to begin a day like any other. Buzzing, buzzing, buzzing, while the whores and the thieves are sleeping.

A few more steps, and Anna comes to a halt and sits down. Her ribcage is clenching, her eyes burning. She knows precisely why she's doing this to herself, why she cannot rent a room in a nice house, one that has a housekeeper with manners instead of a gin problem, one that is clean and even warm in winter. One without death, disease, and violence surrounding her. 'No use to ask yourself that same damned question again,' she growls at herself.

Two large boots come to a halt in front of her. Without looking up she says, 'What do you want, Garret?'

He clears his throat. 'Saw you sitting here and thought you might be needing something.'

'Do you have a cigarette?'

'Hum…' He grunts, one foot tapping indecisively. 'In a minute, for sure.' He dashes off and Anna considers running the other way. But she's too tired, and she'd have to bump into him another day and possibly explain herself. Hoping he won't start a brawl with someone who looks funny, she remains sitting.

A few moments later, Garret returns. His chest is heaving from the run. He fumbles with tobacco and paper, then holds out a cigarette to her.

The fine golden down on the back of his hand looks cleaner than the day he had stumbled into her room. He has looked cleaner ever since. She squints at him. Does he wash regularly?

'Thank you,' she says, moving to the side a little so he can sit if he likes to.

The doorsteps are a little too narrow for both of them, but he squeezes in nonetheless.

'You look tired,' he says.

She leans her chin onto her palm and watches the fog rise. 'Look.' She points, and Garret watches the everyday spectacle as though he has never seen it before. Tendrils waft into the street, covering puddles with delicate frosting, then grow thicker until a breeze pushes them back to where they came from.

'You have shit on your shoes,' he observes.

'I have been at Clark's Mews.' She bends down and unlaces her boot, pulls it off, and whacks it against the wall. 'Dammit,' she mumbles.

'Let me try.'

She gives her shoe to Garret, and he whacks and whacks until the last bit dislodges. 'Thank you,' she says, putting her boot back on.

Tobacco smoke mingles with rising fog and the stink of the Thames. Anna sees herself with the eyes of her colleagues — a cigarette touching her lips without a tip separating the unwomanly thing from her skin, her hands are gloveless, her hair short, her shoes stink of excrement. None of the good doctors would recognise her, should they ever dare place their lacquered boots in this part of London.

'Want me to bring you home?' he asks.

'If you are in need of a woman, go this way.' She points to where she has just come from. Her tone, devoid of emotion, cuts him deeper than fury.

'That's not what I meant!' His orange hair sticks out in all directions as though indignation has shot lightning through his skull.

'What do you mean, then? You want me to believe we *accidentally* run into each other every so often? I'd never seen your face until the day you fell into my rooms, bleeding all over the place. Now I see you almost every evening. Why is that?'

40

'Only mean to protect you,' he grumbles, rising to his feet. 'You saved my life. You don't belong here; you don't *need* to be here, and everyone knows it. Some are just waiting to take advantage of you.'

She sees his broad shoulders sag and feels an odd urge to apologise, or at least explain. 'A girl's mouth had been slit open because she didn't want a cock in it. The man didn't take the time to notice or even care that she is only a child.'

Garret sits back down and, not knowing what might be the appropriate thing to say, takes her hand into his, sucks at a corner of his shirt, and uses the moist thing to rub a speck of blood off her wrist.

'Why are whores wretched, I wonder. Seems like a rule: whores are wretched. Even the ones that do the gentlemen,' he muses and inspects both her hands for more blood, but finds none. 'Maybe men leave their wretchedness inside a whore. Cleanse themselves of it, in a way.'

'Don't tell me you've never had a prostitute.' She extracts her hand from his grip.

'I didn't say that, did I now?' He presses his lips to a thin line. 'I never believed I owned them! Don't want to be owned by anyone myself. Always trying to treat others the way I want to be treated.' He clears his throat. 'I'm lucky. No one would take me serious with that soft head of mine if it were set on a normal body.'

'It works. You scared me,' she confesses.

'Didn't mean to. I mean, scare *you*.'

41

They watch a cat cross the street. Her ribs grind against the inside of her coat, shoulder blades pointing toward the night sky. The moonlight cuts her bony outlines onto the pavement. She steers towards them until a rodent sticks its nose too far out of a piece of banged-up piping. As the cat jumps, it is as though two black cats separate, one in the air, one street-bound. A moment later, they touch paws again.

'Men hate whores because they show us what we are,' says Garret.

Anna opens her mouth and shuts it again.

'They know we are a herd of horny monkeys with a variety of appetites,' he adds.

The *crunch crunch* of cat teeth on rodent bones is barely audible over Garret's low voice. Whatever kind of judgement was forming in Anna's head topples into nonexistence with these two sentences of his.

'Whores serve as a refuse heap,' she begins. 'A set of arms to weep in, a lover, sister, mother, child, punisher. Whatever a man needs, he can buy it for a few shillings, maybe a sovereign if it's *special*. Thousands of whores live in this city. They are doomed to die early, be it from disease, from sloppy abortions, or from having been used so often that their souls bleed out their orifices.'

'You don't hold men in high esteem,' Garret says.

'I don't hold pretence in high esteem.'
'What do you... You don't think I...'

'No!' She slams a fist against her forehead. 'Simple calculation: there are about eighty thousand whores in London, all receiving between three and ten customers each day. That makes a lot of Londoners lying in the arms of someone they despise in public.'

A flock of street urchins hurries past them. Their squeals of delight seem to be directed at a man who has just entered the street. There, where the lone lantern stands. The gleaming silver knob of his walking stick betrays his idiocy. The thing is whacked from his hand, his clothes are tugged off, and only seconds later, all he's left with is his birthday suit.

Anna rubs her brow. She is struck by an oddity. People here are saving their non-existent money by sharing rooms. They are honeycombing themselves and their meagre belongings into rooms the size of a cupboard. Yet, Garret has his one mattress, his one hook on the wall, his one creaky chair all for himself. When she asks him about it, he falls silent for a long moment, and she begins to think her question might have been too private.

Then, he finally answers. 'I don't understand most people. And I *like* living alone.'

Anna's head turns, her eyes glued to a man she doesn't know a bit.

'Besides...' He breaks off, his face heating with shame.

'What?'

He coughs and shakes his head. 'It's...embarrassing.'

'Oh.' She'd like to know what's so embarrassing, but doesn't want to press him. At least not directly. She puts her chin into her hand again and traps his gaze with hers. It takes a while, but shows effect.

'Can you keep it?' Forget-me-not eyes blink at her.

'I will,' she answers, and adds in her mind, *I keep so many secrets that sometimes I don't know where I left my head.*

'I...read.'

It takes her a moment, but puzzle pieces fall together eventually. 'The dangerous Irish thief cannot be seen with his nose in a book. People would think him a harmless freak. Who taught you how to read?'

'My father. He wanted to give me the farm when I'm old enough, so he taught me bookkeeping and all.'

'What are you reading?'

He shrugs. 'Um...books?' She squints at him, and he shrugs again. 'This and that.'

He doesn't want to say that he reads what he finds in the houses he burgles. 'The one I'm trying to read now makes me all cross-eyed. From some idiotic fella named Percy Shelley.'

He turns his head away.

'Why are you ashamed?' Her voice is like a soft caress, trickling down his spine. He feels a sudden urge to press his face to her bosom. Instead, he gazes towards the one lit lantern, far down the street, where a naked man holding his crotch staggers out of the yellow light.

'I told you so you wouldn't think I'm a stupid brute. But now that I told you, *I* think I'm a stupid brute.'

'I don't like that Percy fella, either,' she says with a smile. 'Try Mary Shelley next time. And no, she's not related to Percy. She's all together different material.' With that, she rises and touches his shoulder as a farewell, knowing precisely he would insist on leading her home safely.

The Girl

The stairwell is dark this time and the steps seem to be creaking louder as Anna ascends to the second floor. The women go about their usual business and only one is in bed without company. Anna knocks and — not expecting an answer from the severed mouth — she enters. 'Hello.'

The girl sits on her bed, her shoulders squared, chin set. Her face is swollen; black silk threads stick out of the wound, giving her a monstrous, tilted grin.

'How are you doing? You can nod or shake your head, no need to speak.'

'I can sheak,' she answers slowly. ''Ust'nt use sone 'ords.'

'I'm relieved,' says Anna and places her palm on the girl's forehead. 'You have no fever. Good. How does the wound feel?'

The girl's face begins to glisten.

'You are my patient. I'm bound to never mention a word to anyone about your condition or what circumstances led to it. That includes your madam,' Anna says.

Considering, the girl's eyes glide out of focus for an instant. 'I'n alright.'

Anna tips her head in reply. 'I'll examine your wound and give you something to speed up the healing process. If anything I touch hurts a lot, you must tell me. Otherwise, I might miss an infection that could kill you. Do you understand?' She tries to make her voice soft.

The girl nods.

Anna disinfects her hands, dabs a little iodine on the wound, and gently probes with her fingers. Clear liquid exits the ragged cut. 'Open your mouth, please.'

Her lips are parting just a fraction. With an *uhnf,* she closes her mouth and shakes her head.

'I know,' says Anna. 'Can you try an inch? I need to take a quick look only.'

The girl's eyes get glassy when she opens up her mouth, the fingers of one hand pressing against the corner of her lower lips to lessen the tension on the suture.

Anna twists her neck to peek through the small opening. The girl's teeth are two curved rows of pearls in a tortured oyster.

As gently as possible, Anna inserts two fingers into the girl's mouth, moves the tongue aside, and uses her other hand to hold a candle close enough to see the inside. The cheek looks raw and inflamed. 'Did you eat anything?' she asks when she cleans her hands on a handkerchief.

The girls shakes her head.

'I thought so.' Anna pulls a bunch of dried camomile from her bag. The valuable disinfectant would be taken from her patient in less than an hour, while camomile is but a weed of no particular interest. 'Can you walk around and make yourself tea from this?'

She nods.

47

'It is important that you wash your mouth at least five times a day with camomile tea. The inflammation will go away, and the pain, too.'

The girl nods.

'What happened?' slips out of Anna's mouth.

Shame begins to colour the girl's face. 'Scared 'ee.' Her eyes water, she shakes her head as if to get rid of the memory, then she lies down and stares at the ceiling.

Anna watches her unmoving figure for a long moment, then touches her arm. 'You will be better soon.'

The girl turns her face away.

Anna rises and makes to leave. When she holds the doorknob in her hand, she hears a whisper from the bed. 'He loohes his knihhh.'

Returning to the bed, she asks, 'He loves his knife?' and receives a nod in return. 'How do you know?'

'Ex…Ekhen'ive.'

'Expensive?'

Another nod.

''Other of 'earl handle. He did…' The girl lifts her right hand, her index finger and middle finger straight out like a blade. She caresses her face with the pointy tip, slides it down her throat, around her breasts, down her stomach where her knife-hand compacts to a trembling fist.

'Did he cut you there?' Anna asks, but knows the answer already. There was no blood leaking from the girl's vagina last night. 'Are you still a virgin?'

The girl nods again.

Behind her back, Anna curls her one hand around her other compacted one, but the tension won't lessen. 'The madam will let you stay here. I'll come back tomorrow.'

Descending the stairs, she tries to make sense of the little information she got. He must have asked for a virgin, for they are kept for the highest bidding customers. Was he a regular? Surely he must have paid for silence.

The corridor to the parlour is blocked by the madam. 'The girl wouldn't speak a word,' Anna lies. 'I examined her. Her wound will heal in due time. And she's still intact.'

'Good,' grunts the woman and crosses her arms over her chest. 'We can't pay you.'

'You sold the virginity and health of one of your girls to a rich man only yesterday. Some of that money must still be in your possession.' Anna holds out her hand and does something she's never done before. 'I have to charge five shillings.'

Narrowed eyes pierce hers.

'Make that a half-sovereign and you'll keep your mouth shut,' the madam says.

Hot blood rushes up Anna's face. 'Since the man paid for a virgin but didn't deflower her, will he return and ask for the money back, or will he ask for the services he paid for?' She drops her hand.

The madam calls over her shoulder, 'Butcher! Our guest wishes to leave.'

A man emerges. The nickname does him justice. His body is made for lugging halves of pig and cattle, his eyes are empty.

'Ma'am,' he says.

'I will be back tomorrow,' Anna says. 'Should the wound get infected, the girl will die.'

She leaves the brothel, wondering yet again why anyone had the need to cutify this place by calling it a boarding house. A bitter taste constricts her throat until Clark's Mews is out of sight.

***

Garret strikes another match on his boots, then searches the tall shelf. He is about to grow impatient when his eyes finally fall on "Shelley. *Frankenstein.*" He pries the volume — gently held by books on either side — from its place, opens it, and whispers, 'Hello, Mary,' then slips it into his shirt and proceeds with his primary goal.

Strongboxes — or rather, their preferred hiding places — infected Garret with a love for stories. Often, he had to search the library, or the sitting room, if it wasn't a too-well situated household he burgled, to find the strongbox hidden behind books. Sometimes, when he was lucky, a larger strongbox was concealed by a panel of fake spines.

Once he followed a whim and picked up a slender book that was beautifully bound in fine leather with golden letters crawling across it. He was far from wanting to read it. To him, it looked valuable.

And valuable it was. When he arrived at his room and stashed away his loot, he thought it couldn't cause any harm to see if the pretty book contained anything entertaining. He'd never heard of Walt Whitman. But the following morning he awoke with his nose and cheek pressed flat against "I am large, I contain multitudes." Drool had smudged the ink, giving him a somewhat reasonable excuse to not sell Mr Whitman to the duffer.

Now, Garret makes to pry open the strongbox before him. This particular specimen had been hiding at the very top of the shelf, behind a disorderly stack of encyclopaedia, papers, and magazines. He'd had to climb a chair to find it, and the combined weight of burglar and strongbox make the furniture underneath him creak.

He places the box on the rug, squats down, and inserts one of his slender cast iron tools into the first lock. He listens intently. Not only for noises that would indicate the house's inhabitants are awake and possibly aware of his presence; he's also listening for the soft clicking and scraping of lockpicks against levers. He works with fingertips and ears, his eyes half-closed, his head tipped as though to place a kiss on a lover's brow.

It doesn't take long and Garret moves on to the second lock. *How stupid*, he thinks. If he would ever have cause to protect his valuables in a strongbox equipped with two locks, he would not use identical ones and certainly not use locks that had two levers only.

In less than three minutes, Garrets cracks the thing and opens the lid. He strikes another match. A smile flits across his face when light is reflected by sapphires and gold. He'll have to hide the jewellery for at least six months, until the police have given up searching for it. He takes it all — it's not much, fitting snugly into his large palm — then wraps it into strips of cloth together with his cracksman equipment and rises to his feet to leave.

It always gives him a stomach ache when he places valuable loot together with his tools. In his whole career as a cracksman, he had to drop the package twice, and only once was he able to retrieve it from the muck of the Thames. But it would have cost him his freedom, perhaps even his life, had he not rid himself of evidence.

Tonight, no one disturbs him. He exits the villa through the back door and walks home as though he is taking a casual stroll. His heart is thumping a little faster than normal. Partially with the excitement the adventure brings, partially with hope. The jewellery will allow him an above-average lifestyle for months, perhaps even a year. Above St Giles average, to be specific, once he has turned gems and gold into money.

Rarely a day passes without him dreading the hovels he once called home. He had been fourteen or fifteen years old, had just fled to London, and lived with several other inhabitants in a too-small room. The place reeked, and not even a wide open window could reduce the stink to a bearable level. Rotten food was squeezed in between the floorboards' cracks — floorboards so dirty that one must think they'd never seen a brush in their entire life.

Twelve pallets with mouldy straw mattresses atop were stuffed into the limited space. He had to climb over sleeping bodies to reach his bed. He can still hear the tinkling of urine in chamber pots, the snoring and grunting, the bawling of an infant, the swearing, burping, and farting. This was not the shiny paradise his once-boyish mind had dreamed up. This was the place where humans had reached their lowest point and had long lost all shame.

The boarders came and went, always too many for the few bedsteads. People had to sleep in shifts — half of them during the day, the other half at night. Whenever Garret returned from his nightly thieving adventures, heat rose up his cheeks just before he pushed the door open. There was no privacy when poverty was as severe as it was here.

He can still taste the bile on his tongue when images of that particular night flit unbidden past his retinae. He had just returned with Mr Strike — his so-called mentor — from burgling a shop. In the light of his oil lamp, he saw an elderly man and a young woman coupling on a palette in the middle of the room. The flimsy cover barely concealed the man's wrinkly buttocks. In the far corner, a girl smiled up at Garret when he stepped through the door. Her face was reddened, her skirts hiked up, and her fingers fluttered through the dark triangle between her legs. Upon her inviting nod, the adolescent Garret chucked his brain on the nearest refuse heap.

The resulting pregnancy ended in an early and rather bloody miscarriage and in Garret avoiding cramped quarters at all costs.

Disappearance

She knocks at the door and it takes a while until someone answers. Butcher's face shows in the crack. 'What do you want?'

'Same as yesterday.'

'She left this morning.'

Suspicion tingles Anna's neck. 'Where did she go?'

He snorts. 'Her mother.'

'Where is that?'

'How would I know? Now get off the doorstep.'

'I don't believe a word,' says Anna.

'Not my problem.' The door shuts in her face. She remains standing. Her eyes trace the cracks in the wood. One part of her wishes the girl had left to a mother who cares for her. The other part knows that one doesn't simply leave home to go straight to the most wretched whorehouses in London. Women end up here when they have nowhere else to go. Girls end up here when their parents have sold them, or a professional seducer has lured them away.

A window creaks open. The contents of a chamber pot descend along the wall, yellow trickling over dull grey. A head sticks out the window and Anna recognises one of the women who had held the injured girl two nights ago. Before she can call up to her, the woman presses a finger to her lips, then signals Anna to wait.

Two minutes later, she is at the window again, drops a crumpled piece of paper, and hisses, 'Leave!'

Anna picks up the message and disappears down the street.

***

'What's up?' a low voice inquires over the singing and brawling produced by semi-drunk clientele.

'Hello, Garret.' She slips the message into her sleeve and turns towards him.

'You look…sad?'

'Hmm…' she says, eyeing her food.

'If you want me to leave you alone… Erm… Do you want me to leave?'

She looks up at him, crinkles her brow, and shakes her head. 'Want an ale?'

'Sure.' He slumps down next to her. 'What are you doing here, anyway?'

'Eat. Drink.' She indicates the yet-to-be-eaten meat pie and the almost-finished glass of brandy. Carefully, she picks at the pie, its inside steaming hot, and puts a piece into her mouth. She sees Garret's eyes dart to her plate, then tearing himself away from it. 'Two more,' she shouts at the landlord and points to her food. 'And an ale.'

Soon, the requested items are placed in front of her, baked pork aroma wafting from it.

She pushes the new arrivals to Garret. 'I don't like to eat alone.' *With someone drooling on my sleeve*, she adds silently.

'Thanks.' Garret stuffs half a pie into his mouth. 'Oufff!' he hisses, then sucks in air to cool his scorched tongue. He swallows and says, 'You got a secret message. What does it say?'

'If I would tell you, it wouldn't be secret, would it?'

'It would be a secret between you and me.'

'I don't share secrets with you.'

'Hrm,' answers Garret and puts more pie into his mouth. She watches him chew on his food and her rejection.

He shrugs. 'Just thought you might need help from an accomplished cracksman.'

'What's a cracksman?'

'A burglar.'

'Is that your speciality?'

'Best in the neighbourhood.' He slaps his chest, blushes, and returns to eating.

Anna wonders whether he might indeed be able to help. 'Finish your food,' she says and puts money on the counter, nods at the landlord, and rises to her feet.

Big-eyed, Garret grabs the last pie, tips the entire ale down his throat, and follows her outside.

The door of the "Dog and Rat" slams shut and the two walk until they find a quiet place. 'If you wanted to find a man, how would you go about it?'

Surprised, he cocks his head and squints down at her.

Her cheeks grow hot. 'God, no, Garret!' she cries and slaps her forehead.

'What man?'

'I don't know his name.'

'What do you want from him?'

'Ah,' she begins, her eyes searching the pavement for the proper words. 'He's hurt a girl. Cut her face open with a knife. The girl disappeared. The man will probably not come back. I want to know what happened to her and whether he somehow…made her disappear.'

'Oh, that fella,' grumbles Garret, and Anna's heart hollers a wild *thump thump*.

'You know who he is?' she asks.

'Of course not. Never seen his face. But I heard things.'

'What things?'

'Well-to-do fella who likes to run his knife over bare skin. Likes to leave marks. Nothing serious. Just…scratches.' Garret stuffs his hands in his trouser pockets and looks at his shoes.

'What else?'

'People say that…that he likes it when women are bleeding. The monthly…thing.'

'Menstruation,' she supplies, trying not to slap her head again.

'Yeah, that.'

'Does he fuck them or is he only using his knife?'

Her words shake off Garret's timidity. 'I don't know.'

'Can you find out?'

He takes a step towards her. 'You will not get near this fella.'

'Why not?' She crosses her arms over her chest.

'How naive are you?' he almost shouts.

'Quite naive,' she answers. 'Do you know who he is? Or how I can find him?'

'What's on that message you hid in your sleeve when I entered the pub?'

'Nothing of interest,' she says.

'Very well, then. If you don't tell me, I won't help you.'

She smoothes the front of her skirt, nods, and walks away.

'Dammit!' she hears Garret growl. Footfalls approach and he is at her side again.

'What happened to your sister?' she asks to distract him.

He stops and gapes at her, then opens his arms wide in puzzlement. 'She...died.'

That worked well, Anna scolds herself when Garret turns and walks away. She increases her speed and touches his arm. 'I am sorry.'

He pulls up his broad shoulders, then lets them slump. 'She had consumption. Mother still had years 'til she died. But my sister...' He sighs and comes to a halt. 'Ena was only four. It was quick.'

His brow in crinkles, he nods decisively, then sets one foot in front of the other again.

59

Anna touches his elbow. 'Thank you for offering your help.'

'Yeah,' he answers and trots on. He stops at the front door to her home, takes her hand and squeezes it, then says, 'You will not find the girl, Anna.'

'Why do you believe that?'

'What do you think happens to a whore who's of no use to the madam?' he asks softly, as though the truth, if spoken harshly, could knock her out.

'She's still a virgin,' she protests. 'She has perfect teeth. Only that scar—'

'Listen to yourself!' Garret barks. 'Whores pay rent for the room they live in, fuck in, and wash their customers' juices from their quims! If she cannot take a man, she cannot pay rent. She'll be thrown out. That girl's face is a mess! Everyone knows she didn't want a cock in her mouth. She isn't worth a farthing!'

At his last word, Anna slaps him hard in the face.

'Dammit! That's *not* how I meant it!' he growls, holding his stinging cheek.

'How did you mean it, then?' she snarls back at him.

'To the madam, she has no value. That girl didn't leave. She got kicked out, and another girl will take her place tonight. Probably already has.'

They stare at each other. Anna knows he's correct. She pictures herself showing up at the Bow Street Police Station and telling the bobbies a prostitute has disappeared. They'll laugh, clap her shoulder, and tell her that this happens every day. Whores move to another madam, go back home to their mothers, or to a workhouse. Who cares? The police would probably tell her it was the girl's own fault that a customer lost control when she wouldn't satisfy him.

Anna sighs. 'I know. And yet…'

'And yet,' he agrees. 'You wish you could use your head to bang a hole through the wall.'

She graces him with a smile, softly places her hand on his reddened cheek, then disappears through the door.

The stairs up to her room seem unusually steep tonight. She locks her room and gazes through the window until Garret's back disappears. Then she spreads the crumpled note on the kitchen counter.

5ft 9   180 lbs

fair hair

~~thin~~ moustache

scar on left hand

'Useless,' she mutters, wishing she could return to Clark's Mews and shake all required information out of the woman.

Herbs

Somewhere far away, church bells are banging. Respectable people get themselves a set of painful knees each while praying in church pews someplace other than St Giles. Here in the slums, morals have left long ago, or never actually arrived in the first place. Hence, this is no place for God-fearing folk. Or so the God-fearing folk believe.

Crossing the street and not even thinking of wasting her time with prayer, Anna bumps into Garret.

'Oy, Anna! Where're you heading?' He eyes her rucksack.

'Outing,' she provides through a bit of apple in her mouth.

'Did you hear that Maclean tried to kill the queen?' Garret begins in the hope she'll stay a little.

'That was in March.' She stops, swallows, and looks up at him in puzzlement. 'Three years ago.'

'I know.' He pulls his eyebrows together. 'I was just trying to chat you up.'

His honesty and drooping shoulders make her laugh. 'I took a holiday. I want to collect medical herbs.'

'What? Where?' His face lights up from the unusually large amount of personal information she provides.

She smiles — more to herself than to anyone else and walks ahead.

Feeling oddly invited, he trots along.

'I'll take the train from Victoria Station down to Purley. It'll be a nice day in the countryside.'

As though it needed checking, Garret looks up into the pale blue sky and nods, then sets eyes and nose at the potato man selling his wares out of his basement window. 'Did you have breakfast?' he enquires.

'Yes,' she says, and waits while he haggles for a particularly large and steamy specimen, which he begins to devour at once.

As they commence their stroll, Anna observes the man next to her and her reactions to him. Her fear of him has long disappeared. The curious mix of hard-boiled wisdom and child-like naivety, his heart at the tip of his tongue whenever they meet, make her feel safe. She feels respected despite his urge to protect her. He often appears out of nowhere, obviously keeping an eye on her, but all he has ever tried in terms of approach was to hold her hand. Whenever she withdraws it, he usually doesn't pick it up for the remainder of the day. Not once has he attempted a kiss, a hug, or a touch anywhere other than her hand. 'Thank you,' she says softly.

'Huh?' he grunts through baked potato stuffed between his teeth.

'For your company.'

His food lands in shrapnels on the pavement as he blurts out, 'Fo Furley, foo?'

'Would you like to come?' She knows exactly that he does, but she wants to make him talk with a full mouth once more.

He nods. 'Offcorffe!'

She tugs him along, tilting her face away from him to hide a smile.

The train is full and the two remain standing close to the door. At their feet is a stack of three small cages, four chickens squeezed into each one of them. Garret sticks out of the crowd because of his height, and Anna because of her hair. He tugs at a curl. 'Why did you cut it so short?'

'Because I wanted to,' she says, and myriad memories roll over her. She looks up at Garret, and for the first time she feels a little sorry that she cannot tell him who she is. 'Garret?' she whispers and he lowers his head to hear her better over the rattling of wheels, chatter of passengers, and clucking of hens. She leans into him and sees his pupils dilate, his gaze travelling down to her lips. 'There is a lot I cannot tell you about me.'

His urgent need to kiss her evaporates. He straightens up and looks out the window, sees London fly by, and curls his arm around the woman he suddenly fears to lose, although he'd never had her to begin with.

Surprised, she notices that his arm feels warm and pleasant where it rests. Her brain begins to scold her, lists the reasons why she shouldn't let him get so near. Her heart, however, beats quicker and lets her know that she's a human made of brain

64

and heart and flesh and soul — wouldn't it be a waste to nourish only part of oneself?

She lets the two sides argue and decides to form an opinion some other time.

Unspeaking, Garret and Anna walk out of Purley Station and through the small town out onto the meadows. He lies down in the grass and gazes up at the clouds while she picks yarrow and ribwort. Gradually, she drifts towards him and soon joins him in the shade of a lime tree. He watches her slender figure stretching up to pick blossoms from the tree. Finally, he dares to ask the question that has kept him silent for the past hour. 'How often did you lie to me?'

'Often.' A matter-of-fact voice, directed not at him but at the tree — mute, safe for the buzzing of hundreds of bees.

He observes her calm moves, her set chin, and knows she won't budge.

'Why am I here?' he asks.

She feels a stab in her chest, one that expels all air from the lungs and makes her realise that what she is choosing now will one day destroy their friendship, should they ever have one. Do they have one, already? Perhaps they do.

She drops her linen bags in the grass and sits down next to him. 'When we met for the first time, you were but a stranger. Why would I reveal my secrets to a stranger?'

He puts this aside with a dip of his chin, then repeats his question. 'Why did you cut your hair short, Anna?'

When she opens her mouth to answer, he interrupts. 'I don't want to hear it if it's a lie.'

'Because I wanted to.' Her voice is soft.

'Have you been in an asylum? Or gaol?'

The most natural conclusion. Women with short hair are either lice-ridden — which she obviously is not — or have spent time as inmates.

'Of course not,' she says indignantly.

He nods. 'Are you married?'

She sees how hard this question is for him to ask. 'No. I'm not married.'

'Are you a widow?'

This is what she has told everyone. She presses her lips together and stares hard at him. 'Garret, for you and everyone else, I am a widow. I will never state anything else, not even here in this remote place. It does not matter whether I was married to him' — *them*, her mind corrects — 'or not. So, please, it is easier if you accept that *I am a widow*. It protects me.'

His eyes widen, then he drops his gaze. 'May I court you, Anna?'

Her innards contract with a jolt. 'No,' she breathes.

He sees her pale face and doesn't know what to make of it. Does he repel her so? But why would she allow him to hold her hand? Was that some kind of lie, too? 'I don't know who you are,' he whispers.

'You know me better than anyone else, save for my father.'

He shakes his head, two slow fractions of a movement. 'Why do you do this? Why all the

66

secrets? No friends? No husband?' He squints, feeling angry, helpless, and at the same time, sorry for her as well.

'If people knew my secret, I'd have to leave England and spend a few years in gaol.'

Garret sits erect like a stick, eyes wide, mouth straining not to gape. 'Did you murder someone?'

'Don't be ridiculous. I would be hanged, not deported.'

'Yeah, true.' He slumps back down in the grass.

'I would like to be your friend, Garret. But you would have to accept me the way I am.'

His eyes light up for a moment at the thought that this woman likes him. Then, heaviness spreads when the realisation sinks in that he might never know her secrets.

He nods anyway.

Testing the newly won freedom, or closeness, or sort-of-honesty, or whatever this is, he dares to ask, 'What was on that note you hid in your sleeve the other day?'

'A rough and rather useless description of the man who injured the girl.'

'You're still looking for him?' He rubs his face and gets all cross-eyed from his impatience with her.

'I believe he's dangerous. The girl said that he loves his knife — an expensive thing, with mother-of-pearl inlays. He ran the blade over her body, even across her vulva. He seems to revel in

67

the terror he causes. But what I really want to know is what happened to *her*.'

He inhales slowly; his chest expands until a grumble pushes though his throat. 'And after that you plan to do what? Save all whores?'

'It's as hopeless as attempting to eradicate all disease. But healing one ailing person at a time, is that not worth the effort?' She sees his face relax. Only a small frown curls his mouth. 'Would you help me, Garret?'

His eyebrows pull together. One might interpret his expression as inviting, so she continues. 'The woman who gave me the note. I'd like to ask her a few questions, but obviously I cannot march into a brothel and interrogate a prostitute. She might lose her room. So I thought…perhaps you could go. As a customer. I'll give you five shillings, if that's what she asks for. I don't even know how much…' She trails off. Garret hides his face in his sleeve.

'You ask me to visit a whore whom *you* pay? Did I just hear that? Did I?' He shakes his head and looks at her.

She nods.

'Goddammit, Anna.' He jumps up, wondering whether he ought to regret this trip to the countryside, but he cannot bring himself to do so. 'Tonight?'

'If it's possible.'

'Do you want me to ask her your questions before or after I used her services?' He wants to shake her by her shoulders, but all he comes up with are acidic words.

'I wouldn't recommend bedding her,' she whispers, the small sores at the corners of the woman's mouth brightly visible in her mind. 'I believe she has syphilis.'

His jaws are working. Not knowing how to reply without shouting or ripping his own hair out, he turns and walks away.

She watches him for a moment, weighing the consequences of her actions. If he walks away from her for good, it might have been worth hurting him.

Garret

𝔇is back presses lightly against a wall. Perhaps a bad idea, considering the daily flow of piss down the plaster. Anna stands next to him with her arms crossed over her chest. 'This is the woman,' she says quietly without pointing. 'Do you know her?'

'Never seen her before.' Garret pushes away from the house and crosses the street. The woman's skirts are frayed, her shirt too loose around her bosom, a scarf conceals nothing and warms nothing. Her face is powdered, her lips painted blood red. A fake smile cracks open her mouth.

'Ten minutes in heaven for only two shillings,' she rasps.

Garret nods towards a dark corner — there, behind that flimsy billboard.

Her face falls. 'I have a room, sir. I'm a respectable woman!'

'No need to call me *sir*,' he grumbles.

She nods, resignation stiffening her moves. His bulk and height frighten her. But then, she always has Butcher who would come at once should this man... On the other hand, Butcher hadn't come when... She stops for a moment, then shakes off the fear. *So what*, her mind rattles, *I've dealt with worse.*

Once in her room, she takes off her shawl to expose more of her shoulders and the flesh of her freckled bosom.

'No need to undress,' says Garrett, lays the fee on the table, and sits down on the only chair in the room. The bed looks too conspicuous to him.

Before he can utter another word, she hikes up her skirts and shows him her bush. 'You are the practical kind. I *do* like that.'

'Bloody Christ!' slips out of Garret's mouth. Shock holds his buttocks to the chair when the woman swings a leg over his knees and purrs, 'Pull the stockings down, dear. They scratch a little.'

To cover her nakedness, he grabs her by her waist and plops her down on his lap. Perhaps a little too abrupt. And perhaps a bad idea, considering the sudden proximity. She squeals in fake delight.

'Listen,' Garret begins in an attempt at gentlemanly behaviour, then swallows when she grinds her privates against his crotch. 'While I very much...' She begins unbuttoning his trousers. '...appreciate the effort...' She tries to extract his manhood from the confinement of his drawers. 'I'd rather ask you a question or two. So if you please, let go of my cock?'

Her head jerks up. 'Yer havin' the clap?'

***

Butcher tips his knitted cap in farewell and Garret is out the door in an instant. He spots Anna's silhouette at the other side of the street. Anger wells up his throat. Not only did she find it utterly natural to ask him to visit a whore — a woman who now believes he has a disgusting disease because all he wanted to do was talk — Anna even insisted on paying for the adventure, and, if the woman didn't have syphilis, Anna wouldn't have cared much whether he used her or not.

Garret feels very dirty all of a sudden. Knowing that her eyes are on him, he pretends to close the last button of his trousers, wiggles and arranges the waistband, then turns on his heels and walks home.

He kicks open his door, grabs a bucket, and walks down to the pump. Back in his room again, he indulges in a very thorough scrubbing until his skin begins to burn. Just before he dunks his head into the bowl, he hears a knock.

'Garret?' she asks softly.

Dammit, woman, his mind bellows, *stop pretending timidity!*

Ignoring the rapping, he vigorously rubs soap onto his scalp. The following handfuls of icy water can't cool his mind a bit.

'Garret, could you please tell me why you are angry at me?'

That one question tips him over the edge. He slaps the flannel into the bowl, crosses the room with two stomps and jerks the door open.

'Because you make me feel naked,' he barks, 'and you don't even care.'

He sees her gaze slip from his face and his wild and sopping wet hair, down along his body.

'You *are* naked,' she observes, just before the door slams in her face.

72

'Balls!' he mutters, 'balls, balls, balls!' and frantically searches for a pair of trousers. He hops into them and opens the door again.

Her arms are protectively crossed over her chest.

His jaws are clenched to forbid his mouth to utter a peep.

'I apologise,' she says hoarsely.

The door opens farther, allowing her to step in.

He observes her moving to the window at the other side of the room, observes her chewing on words, and then, opening her mouth reluctantly. 'Washing doesn't help. Did you not listen when I told you that she has syphilis?' She speaks the last sentence quietly and pleading.

His shoulders sag. 'You are an idiot.' He fetches his towel and rubs his hair dry. 'Don't you want to hear what she said?'

She narrows her eyes, and he can't make anything of her scrutinising expression. 'Garret, are you aware that there is no cure for syphilis?'

His anger gets the better of him. 'I don't even know what you mean with syphi… what did you call it?' he lies.

'Syphilis. Same as the French gout.'

'What? Why didn't you say that earlier?' He stretches his waistband and peeks into his trousers. 'Oh no! It looks like a pink cauliflower!' he cries, doubles over, and laughs and laughs until his chest hurts. He chokes, plops down on the chair, and buries his face in his hands. 'Dammit, Anna. How can you think I fucked her?'

Soft footfalls approach. 'You were buttoning your trousers.'

'Because I was angry at you. You sent me to a whore believing I would use her.'

She comes to a halt only inches from him. 'How would I know you weren't interested?'

'Yeah. How would you know?' He speaks into his hands.

Upon her silence, he lifts his head and gazes at the row of small buttons that adorn the front of her dress. The contours of her hipbones shape the fabric. Her fragility and the rawness of his nerves let him wrap his arm around her waist and press his face to her chest. 'How would you know.'

It takes him only a moment to realise that she stiffened the instant he touched her.

He lets go of her, scoots a few feet backwards, and speaks to his hands. 'She said her name is Rose; she's from Manchester. She seems afraid of large men, or perhaps only of me. She doesn't know the name of the fella in question.'

He squints at Anna, who only slowly recovers from her shock. She rubs her arms as though she's cold. Her face is pale.

'I didn't want to scare you,' he says.

She blinks and shakes her head. 'You…didn't.'

'Don't lie to me, Anna.'

'Memories scared me,' she says, then looks as though she regrets that last statement.

74

'Rose saw the man only once and doesn't remember his face very well. She remembers his hands, though. They were fine and clean, his skin without blemishes, except for a red scar on the back of his right hand. A cut, she believes; about two inches long. He was well-spoken. No one believed he could be dangerous.'

Anna clears her throat. 'Is he a regular?'

'No. Not at Clark's. But I heard from others that he has frequented boarding houses in and around Seven Dials for the past three months.'

'What others?'

'Men. In pubs. They heard it from the whores, and sometimes they saw the marks he left. Nothing serious. Scratches, mostly. Not much worse than flogging, they said. Only…done with a knife instead of a stick.'

'Do you know where he went before he came here?'

He shrugs. 'No. But I can ask.'

Her chest heaves as she rubs her brow. 'Does she know where the girl is?'

'No. But she said the girl calls herself Poppy. Last name might be Briggs, or Higgs. Her mother sold her to the madam a few days ago. Poppy never spoke about her home. She works on the streets now.'

'The madam threw her out?'

He nods. She turns to the window and presses her forehead against the glass.

He sees the trembling of her shoulders. Unsure how to make her feel better, he stands and walks up to her.

'I didn't what to scare you so.' His hand softly settles on her shoulder.

'Thank you for helping me, Garret.' Her voice is fighting for control. 'Good night.' she says when she leaves for the door.

'Good night,' Garret answers when she's long gone.

Anna

She stumbles over the doorsteps; her heart is beating wildly and her chest is clenching painfully. She doesn't understand her reaction to Garret. She doesn't understand why old memories still have so much power. Why did they come with such force tonight, but had not bothered her at all this morning? Where was the logic in her being comfortable with his arm around her waist, and only hours later, a similar gesture makes her feel as though he had thrown himself upon her?

She begins to run. Her boots slam through the dirt and stink and piss of St Giles. Her heart doesn't stop aching. She runs until she reaches Bow Street. The door to the cobbler's is shut, so she tries the back, runs up the stairs and down the corridor. She unlocks the small room at the very end, steps in and locks it, fumbles for the matches, then lights two oils lamps and yanks off her dress.

She hates being scared and being fragile, being at the weaker end of humanity's sexual reproduction scheme, of education, employment, and basic rights. If a scream could make things better, she'd scream until her throat turned numb.

Instead, she sheds her dress, and undergarments, and opens the wardrobe where she keeps her disguise. Only ten minutes later, she's her professional and controlled self: Dr Anton Kronberg of Guy's Hospital.

Calmness settles on her shoulders. She picks at a lock of hair that sticks out from behind her left ear, then adds a bit more Macassar oil until she's satisfied. She places a top hat onto her sleek hair and picks up the ebony walking stick, its silver knob reflecting the dim light.

When she closes the door to her secret dressing chamber and sets out for a late work night in her laboratory, she's glad to leave her female self behind.

Sally

Barry squats at his usual spot, more or less at the usual time. It doesn't take long for Anna to emerge from her house.

'Hello, Barry,' she says.

'Hello, Anna,' he squeaks and tugs at her skirt. Her tired expression makes space for a smile. 'Can you see my mom?'

'Something serious?'

'Umm…don't know. She might be hurting a bit.'

She takes his hand and they make their way down Endell Street, turn into Castle Street and up into Barry's house. There's no door to keep unwanted guests out. But then, only a few would want to enter a place as decrepit as this.

The stairs yield even under the boy's weight. Murmur crawls down along the moist walls when they reach the second floor. Then, they turn right to climb through a gap that once used to be a functional door.

Anna lights her lamp and the boy sends a greeting into the dark room. 'Mom?'

'I told you, it's nothing,' rasps the hunched figure in front of a barricaded window. A child is coughing nearby.

'Hello, Sally,' says Anna and squats down next to the woman. 'Your boy is a bit worried. Are you alright?'

79

The answer is a throaty laugh. 'Alright,' she mutters. 'What does that mean? What does that boy know, anyways?'

She continues a tirade about useless men who impregnated her with that useless boy, and about White Velvet being her only friend. Why anyone would call the cheapest gin White Velvet, Anna couldn't fathom.

Barry stands there, examining the tips of his tattered boots.

'Sally, if you simply tell me what ails you, I can stop bothering you.'

The woman clears her throat and spits on the floor. 'The chemist sold me the wrong bottle.' She waves towards a small bucket that has a narrow hose attached to it.

Anna picks up the bottle from inside the bucket and reads the list of ingredients in the dim lamp light. 'How much of this did you use?'

'Used it only once. Almost ate my quim, blasted stuff that.'

'You used it straight from the bottle? You didn't dilute it?'

'Didn't say anything about that, did he now? Gave me the bottle. Charged a shilling. A shilling!'

Anna turns to Barry and hands him a coin. 'Barry, go fetch vinegar, salt, and fresh water. Water from the pump, not the river. Take this bucket.' She points to another, larger one. 'But rinse it before you fill it.'

She slips the bottle — filled with a mix of chlorine solution and other caustic ingredients — into her doctor's bag and sighs. 'Can you sit at all?'

Muttering to herself, the woman shakes her head. 'Can't work like this. Can't even take them in my bum. Burns like I'd been fucked by a bottlebrush.'

Anna rummages through her bag. She rubs her brow when she realises she's out of ointment. 'I'll take a look at the child with the cough while we wait for your son to return.'

A low grunt indicates agreement of some sort.

The coughing sounds low and wet, and Anna's mind registers symptoms and analyses potential risks and treatments as she approaches. The child is wrapped in rags, but sits upright and tries to get the mucous out of her airways.

'Hello,' Anna says when she sits down on the pallet. 'You know, I lost my mouse. It's a really nice one, with white fur and long whiskers. It likes to hide in armpits and behind ears. Would you help me find it?'

Big-eyed attention flares up. Snots glistens in the lamp light. The child nods and wipes her nose on her sleeve.

Anna sends soft hands across the girl's forehead, she presses on sinuses, pulls eyelids down, and probes lymph nodes. 'She doesn't seem to be here. Are you sure you didn't swallow her?'

Frantic nodding, followed by a coughing attack.

'Could you look into mine? To make sure?' Anna opens her own mouth wide.

The girl looks with one eye, then the other. 'I don't see it. What about mine?' she says and opens up her mouth. Anna lifts her lamp. A rugged landscape of swollen and disfigured tonsils gleams at her. Yellow pus oozes from fissures.

'No mouse there, either. Perhaps she ran back home. Hmm... How old are you?' she asks and gets a shrug in return. 'Where is your mother?'

Another shrug.

Anna guesses the girl to be four — too young to know the difference between gargling and swallowing, and she'd certainly not swallow anything bitter. So camomile tea it will be instead of iodine solution or sage infusion. And ribwort in honey to get rid of the mucous. But she'd have to make a deal.

'Can you wait for a moment while I see to the lady over there?'

Anna's eyes meet Barry's, who seems oddly shaken. She nods at him. 'Thank you,' she whispers in his ear and takes the bucket from his hand. 'I propose a gentlemen's agreement.'

'Another one?' he asks.

'Indeed. Full of honour and glory. But no spitting!' The boy, who had just expelled a load of saliva onto his palm, now wipes it on his trousers and reaches out. 'You don't want to hear what I have to propose?'

'Oh.' He pulls his hand away.

'I'll make ointment for your mother, and you see that this girl gets her medicine five times a day.'

They shake hands, Barry pressing as hard as he can. 'Ouch,' says Anna and he grins. They have been at this game for weeks now.

'Sally, I'll mix you a new douche so you can wash the chlorine…the stuff that burns out of you. But the tube has to go all the way in. I'm sorry.'

Sally glares at the small bucket with its attached hose while Anna mixes water and salt to a solution somewhat resembling 0.75 per cent sodium chloride. Then she adds a good dash of vinegar to make it slightly acidic. 'I hold it, you insert it,' she suggests.

Sally fetches her chamber pot, squats down, and hikes up her skirts. With a lot of hissing and grunting, she inserts the tube, then washes the caustic solution from her vagina.

'It will take a while to heal,' Anna says, knowing that this is of no consequence. Sally must make money, and if one orifice hurts more than the others, she'll have to improvise. 'I'll send Barry with ointment. You can take it as needed.'

Sally stands up, drops the hems of her skirts, wipes herself dry, and gifts Anna a decisive nod. She wraps a scarf around her neck and head, then leaves the room without a word.

Anna realises that the woman's other problem is her reputation. A conspicuous itch on the pricks of her customers would result in her being branded a wasp — a prostitute infected with venereal disease. There is little that can be worse for business.

'Would you help me make the ointment?' she asks Barry, knowing the boy is only too eager to leave.

Ointments

She holds out the bucket to Barry, who grabs it and dashes out of her room. When he returns, she has already stoked the fire and arranged a variety of items: a small pot, jars and bottles, and a polished oak stick are waiting on the kitchen counter.

The boy pours the water into the washbowl, rolls up his sleeves as far as they'll go, and offers Anna the soap. She scrubs her hands and forearms, then it's Barry's turn. He's so dirty that the water turns a dark grey, as does the towel he uses to dry himself off.

Silently, he watches and waits for her instructions.

Anna pours almond oil into the pot, sprinkles two tablespoons of dried calendula petals into it, and places it onto the stove. She turns the handle to Barry. 'It needs to be warm, but mustn't get hot.'

'How warm?' the boy asks.

'Warmer than your hand, but you should be able to touch it without burning yourself.'

The boy nods, wraps a towel around the pot handle, and gently swirls the oil, holding it a bit higher above the flames.

Anna breaks small bits off the compressed honeycomb she keeps in a jar on her kitchen cupboard, then adds them to the oil. 'Once the wax dissolves, you can take the pot off the fire.'

They watch the petals release their yellow pigments into the potion while the honeycombs begin to shrink. Barry is all focus and removes the pot when he believes it's time. He sticks his cleanest finger into the liquid, frowns, and walks to the washbowl to lower the pot into the tepid water. A soft hiss and the cast iron loses its heat.

After a minute of swirling and sticking-in fingers, he's satisfied and places the pot on the counter.

Anna observes the boy, his silence, his avoiding of her gaze. She knows his mind craves the distraction, while his heart is ashamed. It isn't logical to feel ashamed for a mother; one cannot choose one's family. But as usual, the heart doesn't care much for logic. Besides, the boy knows enough about tradition and inheritance to be afraid of ending up like all the other wretches.

Anna wipes off the spoon and sticks it into another jar containing a thick golden paste.

'Lanolin,' the boy murmurs, as though to tick off the list of required ingredients. He likes the smell of it. It makes him think of the countryside, that exotic place far away from London, far from the grime and poverty of the slums, so far that he had never seen it and probably never will.

She hands him the spoon and he stirs the paste into the oil, scrapes the remains off with the oak stick, and keeps mixing and stirring until all the lanolin is dissolved.

Meanwhile, Anna places several empty jars into a row, picks up a small sieve, places it next to Barry, and asks, 'How does the calendula look?'

'Looks ready. All limp and mushy,' he answers and, upon her approving nod, begins pouring the warm liquid into the jars, straining calendula petals and three pale bee larvae that had perished in the honeycomb. Within the hour, the mixture will harden to a smooth paste.

Anna tightens the lids. 'Tell your mother that if she wants to put the paste on the inside, she should use only little of it. But she should use it several times a day until the burning is gone. And this…' She fills a small paper bag with camomile blossoms and selects a jar with ribwort leaves in honey. '…is for the girl with the cough. Make camomile tea with this honey and take care she drinks it and no one takes it from her.'

The boy nods, then makes to leave, but his hand hesitates over the doorknob. Anna knows that gesture. She points to the key on the dresser and says, 'Don't let the hag know.' The *hag* being their secret word for the landlord's wife.

Barry pockets the key and slips out the door.

Later that night, she's woken up by his back pressing against her warm feet. And as so often, she thinks of sending him away to his own mattress, of telling him to stop behaving like a beaten-up dog. But then she lets it go.

Before she falls back asleep, another thought brushes her mind — she has to ask Barry's mother about Poppy.

Scotty

Two old women inhabit the stone steps of Short's Gardens' workhouse. A broken jug, a teapot, and a layer of rags protecting their hides are their only possessions. One of them wears a hideous grey waterproof, fastened tightly around her tall frame. The other huddles underneath a checkered shawl of feeble texture, a wheezing infant in her arms, his head pressing against the warm patch of skin underneath her chin. The young boy is the child of a former fellow Crawler. Being the only one of the female trio who'd had the luck to obtain an occupation, she entrusts the boy to the old woman each day from ten o'clock in the morning to four in the afternoon so she can scour pots and pans at the coffee shop on Drury Lane. In return, the two old women receive boiling hot water to soak their second- or third-hand tea leaves.

No one knows whether Scotty wears anything underneath her waterproof, and no one quite wishes to obtain precise information on that particular topic. Yet — depending on the observer's own state of poverty — the muddy, nondescript substance hanging loosely around her calves might eventually be categorised as under-clothing.

She looks down at her bare ankles and feet peeking freely from underneath her waterproof's skirt, and she can't remember when she'd lost her shoes. Otherwise, her mind is as clear as it can be, for she never drinks a single drop of beer or gin. At the moment, she wishes she could get the taste of mould off her tongue and the odd metallic scraping out of her throat. She sighs when she thinks of the meals she'd cooked for herself and her husband — good meals, with cabbage and, at times, even pork chops. Her mouth waters and she swallows. Mould and metal are still not washed away.

Her gaze slides down to her hands — swollen, red, and smarting from constant exposure to sun and rain, heat and cold, and she wishes they were cut, blistered, and sore from hardest labour instead.

At least it's summer, she tells herself. Even the small boy in her friend's arms appears to be able to live a little longer.

When the church bells strike four in the afternoon, a small wave of energy washes through the pair of beggars, lets them sit more erect while their eyes flicker expectantly towards Drury Lane.

Only a few minutes later, a woman in her twenties approaches. All Scotty and Betty focus on is the small package the woman holds in her hand. Both scoot a little closer to the doorstep's edge and wipe their hands in anticipation.

'Here,' she says, holding out the package and throwing a weary glance at the sleeping child.

While the two old women devour the scraps of old bread, the younger grabs pot and jug, dashes back to the coffee house, fills the vessels with boiling water, and returns to Short's Gardens a few moments later.

Hot beverage is exchanged for a sleepy child. Then, the world of Crawlers and that of a woman with a flimsy roof over her head separate for today.

When the sun sets, Scotty and Betty lean against one another for support and warmth. Should one stir, the other will wake from her dozing. Neither of them has slept undisturbed for as long as they've called these doorsteps their home. Neither of them has ever missed the newest news in St Giles, either.

***

The clopping of hooves so late at night is unfamiliar enough for Scotty to crack her left eye open. She pokes her elbow into Betty's ribs, but the so unkindly addressed only grunts dismissively.

Scotty moves her hindquarters closer to the doorstep's edge and her neck a little father from the warming waterproof to peek out onto the street.

Some fifty yards away, a cab stops. A man alights who doesn't belong, but isn't a stranger, either.

Scotty rubs the goop from her eyes and watches the gentleman cross Drury Lane. He approaches a girl. Scotty knows that girl, too. Although this one's new here, everyone knows her story. It's written in her face, as not to say *carved*.

Hmm, is all Scotty thinks when the gentleman and the girl disappear into a house. One cough later, Scotty retreats to her companion's side to lean her head onto the sharp contours of Betty's bony shoulder.

Scarred

It's been a long and hard day at Guy's Hospital and Anna has been yearning for her bed since the moment she peeled off her male masquerade and slipped into skirts and shirt. Despite her tiredness, a question keeps burning in the pit of her stomach, and so she begins searching the streets for Sally.

At the corner to Mercer Street, she finds her talking to a potential customer. Anna waits for the pair to disappear behind a billboard. After a few moments, they emerge. He drops a coin on the pavement and walks away. How odd. Had she not asked him to pay her in advance? Sally wipes herself with her skirts, bends down, and picks up her fee. Anna decides that it's now or very much later.

'Hello, Sally,' she calls and approaches. The other woman gifts her a listless stare. 'I have a question. It'll take only a minute.'

'What did the boy do now?' Sally asks and spits a glob of what might or might not be saliva on the pavement.

'No. No, he's a good boy. But you know that. I wanted to ask you about a girl. She had a room at Fat Annie's, but now works on the street. She has an injury, a long and fresh cut from the corner of her mouth up along her cheek.' Anna gestures with her finger.

Sally looks left and right, and, to be certain, over Anna's shoulder, too. But no lonely man is in

91

reach to serve as an excuse for not being able to stand here and chat.

'She's been working the area for what might be three or four days now. Very dumb one. Was asking all kinds of stupid questions. *Where can I sleep? What am I supposed to do now?*' Sally's voice is mocking and high. 'Everyone knows she didn't want a cock in her mouth. I told her to stand at the corner over there...' She waves up Little White Lion Street towards the urinals at Seven Dials. '...and when the next one comes, charge twenty pounds for her innocence. Can't ask for more with that face.'

'Is she still working here?'

'Course she is. Just wait. She'll show up sooner or later.' Then, Sally scratches her head. And scratches, and scratches. She pulls a few strands of hair from her scalp, is about to inspect them for infestations of whatever species, but then thinks otherwise. Her company might not be keen to watch the popping of lice between two fingernails.

'Come to think of it... I haven't seen her last night.'

'What about this man who fancies running his knife over women's skin?'

Sally waves dismissively. 'I don't believe he did this to that girl. He's a fine one, he is. An artist, he told me.' Her eyes are getting a little glassy.

'Does he pay well?'

'Twice as much, and doesn't even want to—' She cuts herself off; her focus shifts to the other side of the street.

Anna turns. The large silhouette waves a hand, then pretends to be busy with the contents of his trouser pockets.

'He doesn't even want to do what, Sally?'

'Fuck. He doesn't want to fuck. Only when I have my period. Never hurt anyone, just tickles with that blade of his.' She shoves past Anna and walks towards yet another man spotted in not-too-far a distance. She wiggles her hindquarters and whistles a tune.

Anna huffs and crosses the street.

'Hello, Garret. Sally is busy at the moment.'

'I wasn't waiting for her,' he grumbles.

She rubs her brow and sighs. 'I know. I was trying to make a joke. It was a stupid one, I'm sorry. I was angry, but not at you. Would you walk with me a little?'

Garret's shoulders seem to sag a bit, his feet heavy when he walks next to Anna. 'I'm reading *Frankenstein*,' he says. It sounds as if the words stumble out of his mouth, unplanned.

'Do you like it?'

'Hmm.'

She doesn't ask any more, knowing he'll speak if he wishes to.

They reach her house, and he comes to a halt a few steps away from her door. His brow is furrowed. 'Somehow… I don't know. This story…' His hands go hiding behind his back. 'Did you ask me to read it for a reason?'

'I thought you might like what she writes. What's wrong with this particular story?' she says, wondering what makes him so reluctant.

'Hmm.' He nods. 'I thought you wanted to tell me how much I remind you of the creature.'

Stunned, she scrutinises his expression, his words, and posture. 'Why would you think that?'

His face darkens. 'Because I scare you, or repel you. Perhaps both.'

A large lump closes her throat. She doesn't dare to step closer, to take his hand to comfort him. She tries words, instead. 'I think the creature is the only beautiful person in the whole sad story.'

He tips his head and gazes down at her. To test his theories, he takes a step forward. And another one. He sees her muscles tense up. 'There. Fear,' he says softly.

'Does it have to be fear when I avoid your touch? Can it not simply be disinterest?'

He steps back and nods, but a moment later, he shakes his head. 'I don't believe it. But...you are a woman who knows what she wants. Good night, Anna.' With that, he turns and walks away.

She climbs the stairs to her room, grasping the banister tighter than usual.

Wrong Turn

Angry with himself, Garret kicks at the mushy cabbage that lies abandoned on the pavement. The poor vegetable reacts by disintegrating further and sending bits into all directions. If only he had a better education, more money, and less bulk, then perhaps Anna would like him.

The only thing he might be able do anything about is his budget. The education part is a lost case. And the bulk… Well, there is absolutely nothing he can change about his size or his build. The latter might even get worse with age. He snorts at the thought of squeezing himself into a nice suit. And yet, if this was what she wanted, he would do it.

Determination grips him. He'll be a better man. If nothing else, he'll increase his meagre riches and buy her a ring, or a dress, or whatever women fancy.

He stumbles over his own feet. What precisely does she fancy? Did she ever mention the things she's missing or would like to buy if she had more money?

Garret nods to himself and walks on. He'll find out what it is that makes her happy, and he'll acquire the necessary funds. The jewellery he had stolen last time he burgled a house is enough to feed and clothe him for months, once he can turn it into money. But a home and security for a family is an entirely different thing. He comes to a halt. Does she even want children of her own? What a stupid thought! Of course she does. The way she treats Barry — as though he's her own.

Never one of the greedy kind before, the Irish thief has a grand plan now. He has waited long enough, he tells himself. This one place he once had his eyes on, the one too risky to burgle because of the dogs patrolling the premises, might make him wealthy enough. But not before he makes an investment.

***

He gives himself two days for reconsidering and inspecting his plans from all angles. Then, he pays a visit to the butcher and one to the nearest opium den. All he needs now is a cup of tea, a sandwich and a good nap.

By noon, Garret is snoring on his mattress. By eight o'clock in the evening, he begins his methodological preparations: examining the lockpicks for any rusty spots, followed by polishing and oiling of his tools, testing the functionality of the glass knife and the wood cutter.

After all that is done, he slices the pig liver in two and sticks his knife into each of the pieces. He pries crumbs off the opium cake and stuffs them deep into the pockets he has cut, then wraps the bloody mess into wax paper and washes his hands.

He combs his hair and dresses in clean attire. No one needs to know that he comes straight out of London's worst rookery.

Just past midnight, Garret locks the door to his room. He steers towards Drury Lane, then up to High Holborn. Just when he passes the British Museum, he hears a shrill police whistle and the cry, 'Thief! Stop him!'

Garret has to control himself to not dash into the nearest alley and up the gutters, or into back doors of random buildings. This call isn't for him, and running away will only prove him guilty.

Approaching clatter of boots on cobblestones. His hair bristles with anticipation. Soon, the thief must run past him. But no such thing happens.

'Stop right there,' a voice commands. The naked walls echo the clicks of a revolver being cocked.

Obstructions

Anna uses forceps to pick her obstetrician's utensils out of the pot with boiling water. She lets them dry on an impeccably clean handkerchief, wraps them up, and packs the bundle into her doctor's bag. The clinking of metal reminds her of the first time she performed an abortion. The woman almost fainted from the pain.

'Are you coming?' asks Barry, waiting cross-armed and hungry at the door.

She nods at him and snaps her bag shut.

They pass the pieman and pick up their supper, then walk into Clark's Mews.

Mum is sitting just outside her brothel, a stool underneath her buttocks, a spinning wheel in front of her knees.

Anna regards the madam with a curt nod and receives one in return before she walks through the corridor and into the kitchen. Two young women sit at the table. Nate, a greying man, is standing at the stove, clonking a spoon against the rim of a cast iron-pan. He serves as some kind of scarecrow and, at times, as a cook. When he sees Barry, he scoops stew into a bowl and plops it onto the tabletop. 'Sit,' he says to the boy. 'Now or later?' he asks Anna.

'Later, thank you.' She looks at the two women. The older she recognises, the younger avoids her gaze, picking at her nails.

'I'm Anna,' she says and reaches out her hand.

'Patty,' says the other, slams a fist onto the polished wood, and pushes herself up to her feet.

Anna drops her hand and curls it around the handle of her doctor's bag.

The two women climb the stairs and enter a small room that smells of dust, wet plaster, and chlorine. The sheets appear to be freshly laundered and bleached for the occasion.

'Sit for a moment, please.' Anna waves at the bed. Patty obeys, her hands in her lap are gripping one another for support. 'I noticed the clean sheets. Excellent! You have to keep yourself clean as well. No customers, no douches either. Nothing goes into that vagina for at least a week, else you might die from an infection.' Upon an affirmative nod, Anna continues. 'Have you got the money?'

'Yes, of course.' Patty extracts a half-sovereign from between her bosom. Anna takes it and slips it into one of her shoes.

'I can give you laudanum, if you wish.'

Patty shakes her head; it doesn't surprise Anna.

'When did you have your last customer?'

''Bout an hour ago.'

Anna nods. 'Wash, please, then douche with this.' She hands her a small bottle with dilute iodine solution. 'I'll prepare my instruments in the meantime.'

While she disinfects her hands and places her tools on a clean kerchief, she listens to Patty hiking up her skirts, squatting over a bowl, and washing her privates. Anna has her back turned to her. Privacy is a fragile thing.

The mattress sags a fraction when Patty sits down. 'On my back?' she asks.

'Yes. And please take off your dress and undergarments. Cover your upper body so you do not grow cold.'

Awkwardly, Patty does as she's told, then settles down on the bed, her gaze directed at the ceiling. Anna knows that expression — the woman's focus is drifting to a far-away place, a place she visits when she's in bed with a customer. Anna has stopped wondering why men don't notice. But perhaps they do. Do they fancy this emptiness, or do they confuse it with quiet obedience?

Anna shakes off the thought and rubs her hands until they are warm, so as not to startle the woman when she touches her. 'Please move closer to the bed's edge and prop your feet up. Yes, like this.' She guides Patty's legs to where she needs them.

'I'll examine you first,' Anna says, then presses the fingers of her one hand onto the woman's lower abdomen and inserts two fingers of the other hand into her vagina. Gentle shifting and probing tells Anna that the pregnancy isn't far advanced. End of the third month at the most.

She wipes her hand. 'I'll insert the speculum now. It helps me to see what I'm doing. This will not hurt.' Slowly, she pushes the beak-like instrument into Patty, opens it, and sets its position with two screws. Her gaze flicks from her hands to the nervous tension in her patient's thighs, the bleakness of her expression, and back to her work.

Both women know that once the unwanted child is gone, the cycle will start anew, and there is little to be done about it. For Anna, this is hard to accept. She kills miniature children, knowing that she'll never have one of her own. Every time she holds one in her hand and sees the bloody mess of tiny limbs sliced off the small body, she looks up from between the legs of her patient and sees a woman whom nature simply hadn't considered. Not only are prostitutes at the bottom of society's cesspit, evolution has no regard for them, either. Without the ability to switch off conception when copulation is used to avoid starvation and the survival of the species is of no concern, prostitutes are left at a social and biological dead end.

'I'll insert the cervical dilators now. I'll be as gentle as I can, but it will not feel nice, Patty. Tell me when you want me to take it easier on you.'

There is no nod or any other reaction, so Anna inserts the smallest dilator through the speculum and slowly pushes it into the cervix. Patty's thigh muscles snap to attention. Anna picks up a larger and then an even larger dilator, increasing the pin-prick opening of the cervix to about half an inch.

Patty's face is grey with agony; beads of sweat are forming on her brow. 'I'm almost done,'

Anna says softly. 'I'll use the curette now and terminate your pregnancy.'

She inserts the long metal instrument with a narrow and serrated spoon on its end, then she begins scraping at the uterine walls, feeling precisely where this child must be, and how the sharp edge of her tool gnaws it apart. *Murderer*, whispers her mind. *Oversimplifying idiot*, she whispers back.

Patty's legs are trembling; her hands are white-knuckled fists while Anna pulls out blood and flesh with her curette, again and again.

Then she says, 'It is over,' and wipes off the mess, pushes a towel between Patty's thighs, and covers her with the blanket.

An hour and another abortion later, Anna walks down the stairs, past an ascending couple of whore and customer.

Barry's voice issues from the kitchen; the boy sounds well-fed and tired. She steers herself there and plops down on one of the chairs. A bowl of stew appears in front of her, and a slice of bread with butter follows.

The kitchen is empty save for Barry and Nate. The women are all gone, waiting on the street or working up in their rooms.

'Where's Mum?' Anna asks.

Nate jerks his chin toward the corridor. 'Still outside.' He scrubs the now-empty pan, dunks it into a bucket with greasy water, then dries it with his apron and hangs it over the stove. *Clonk clonk*, it says when rubbing on the other two cast iron pans.

Anna wipes her bowl clean with a piece of bread, takes a sip of tea, and rises to her feet. 'Thanks, Nate.'

The man takes the dish from her, the fingers of his right hand gnarled from age, hard work, and war; the left ones from constantly gripping the handle of his stick. She'd assisted him once, when the old wound had ached so much he could barely walk. But there wasn't much she could do. 'Rest that leg,' she'd said, and Nate had only chuckled.

Barry follows her when she walks through the corridor. The door stands ajar and Mum is still busy with her spinning wheel. Anna holds out the two half-sovereigns. The old woman compresses her lips and pockets the coins. 'So much mistrust,' she mutters. 'Sit for a moment, child.'

Barry plops down on the pavement, his legs crossed, his hands searching his pockets. He finds a half-smoked cigarette and lights it.

Mum gazes up into Anna's face. 'I was talking to you.'

'I'm tired, Mum.'

'I know. Sit down anyways.'

So she sits down next to Barry and snatches the smoke from the boy's hands. 'Wait until you are ten.'

'Might already be ten, who knows for sure?' squeaks the boy.

'Then wait until you look like ten,' she retorts and sticks the cigarette between her lips.

'The obstructions are removed?' asks Mum.

'Yes, their courses should come naturally now. Both will be bleeding lightly for two or three days.'

'I know, you told me about the bleeding before. I'm not *that* old.'

'You wouldn't believe how much the young folk forget. Call for me should their bleeding be heavier than one would expect of a menstruation.'

Mum waves at her in an *I know, for Christ's sake!* way, then holds up the two coins. They glisten in the lantern light. 'You know that I gave this money to them, so they can give it to you, so you could give it back to me. Sounds quite mad, if you ask me.'

The money drops into her lap, tinkling with the up and down of Mum's foot on the spinning wheel's treadle.

'I perform abortions only under this condition. They pay me for my services, then I pay the madam a week's boarding fee for each of the girls. Otherwise they'll take customers too early, will get an infection, and die, because I cannot possibly amputate the lower abdomen!' Anna almost shouts.

The risk of infection was great: unwashed cocks, douches prepared with dirty water. She had performed the procedure on a number of St Giles' prostitutes, and so far, none of them had got ill afterwards. Word was spreading that her abortions were clean — not what many pseudo-midwifes and quack doctors offered.

'I don't charge a half-sovereign per week!' Mum huffs indignantly.

'How would I know?' Anna shrugs and looks at the old woman's hands, one holding a cloud of wool, the other leading the fine strand of twisted fibre through a metal eye and onto the spinning bobbin.

'You should try this,' says Mum.

'What? Spinning?'

'Yes. It's good for you.'

'My apologies, but even I need to sleep once in a while. When I work with a thread, it always involves a bent needle and a copiously bleeding wound.'

'With what did I earn your contempt?'

Anna squints at her.

'Do you believe I sell the girl's souls?' Mum laughs. 'Go home, child.'

Gone

A shimmering skin, cracked at its edges, floats atop the lukewarm brew. Whenever she exhales, her breath brushes across the still surface, rippling the brown film, causing it to flicker in shades of purple and turquoise. She stares down at her hands clasped around the earthen cup, thinking about a man with an orange mane. Frowning, she takes a sip. The bitter tea constricts her throat.

Her neighbourhood appears empty without the large man in it. Garret had been a constant factor, the rock in the surge who would be there when needed without demands for himself. Almost too easy to ignore.

The ache that followed his unexplained disappearance astounds her. She must have hurt him badly. *Did he fancy me so?* she wonders for the hundredth time, then shakes her head. It doesn't matter, she reminds herself. Whatever Garret's feelings are for her, she can't reciprocate them, and certainly can't reveal her secret to him. It would be like tipping out a bucket of the absurd and mad.

And yet... Wasn't it society that never allowed her to be what she is and thus forced her to bend herself almost impossibly, to live with all these lies? Garret would never understand. But would *she* want to know what he does, when and where he burgled a house? Of course she would. Knowledge is better than ignorance, no matter how terrible the lore. Perhaps she could share the one half of her life with him and keep the rest in the dark.

'Share?' she wonders aloud, and her flat hand hits the tabletop. What does that entail? Surely he wouldn't be content with a mere friendship. No need to be naive. The thought of Garret naked, expecting her to be sexually receptive, feels like a punch in her face.

'Bollocks!' she scolds herself. She told him what had to be said, and his reaction was appropriate and acceptable. He'll find a good woman. Yet, with him gone, she finds herself missing his humour and happiness, his rough hand holding hers.

Anna slams her cup down; tea erupts from it and lands on the kinked wood.

She stands and gazes out of the window. The summer sun has long set. Outlines of rooftops are black against a dark violet. She lets the spilled tea dry on the table and walks over to Garret's place, knocks on his door, presses her ear against it. If only the silence didn't hurt so. For a moment, she wishes she knew how to pick his lock so she could find clues to his whereabouts. Frustrated, she kicks at the door and turns to leave.

'What ya doing there?' a woman calls from the ground floor.

'I'm looking for Garret O'Hare. Have you seen him recently?'

'And who are ya?'

'My name is Anna Kronberg. I'm a nurse. I treated Garret's wounded leg and he still has my bandages. I need them back. Would you be so forthcoming and unlock his door for me so I can get them?'

'Cunningham's the name,' says the woman, grabbing the banister and beginning to heave herself up the stairs. 'Heard about ya. Yer a good lass. But ya need to use tha' brain o' yers. Heard 'bout ya going inter tha' mad house the 'ther day.' Tutting and huffing, she reaches the top and, after throwing Anna a stern look, opens the door to Garret's room.

Anna's first glance tells her that Garret hasn't packed. The coat hangs on its hook, the bed has its crumpled cover, an oily rag adorns the table.

She walks to the cupboard and opens a drawer, then the next. No lockpicks. But she isn't sure if he even keeps them here. Nonetheless, she feels cold crawling up her arms. Has Garret gone out to burgle a house and not come back?

'When have you last seen him?' she asks the woman.

'Bit more than a week ago. 'E dinna pay his rent.'

'I'll pay it,' Anna says automatically.

A hand shoots out, palm up. The landlady won't let an opportunity like this pass. A sovereign drops into it; gold falling on wrinkly skin coated with soot and potato peel grime. The shiny thing is instantly hid inside a compacted fist.

'That should suffice for three months,' Anna guesses aloud and bids her farewell.

With worry twisting her stomach to a knot, she walks down to the street. *Dead or imprisoned,* is all she can think. No other explanation presents itself.

Man in the Mirror

'William,' his wife cries for the fourth time. 'Take your toys to your room and go to bed!' The man hears the rustling of her dress, the clacks of her heels as she walks with swift strides, the whispers exchanged between her and the governess. His fingertips slide along the edge of his collar and fold them down over the cravat. His wife should have done this. He takes the top hat from his manservant's gloved hands, sets it atop his scalp, and regards himself in the looking glass once more. What he sees is a respectable man who is on his way to the opera. He tries a smile. The corners of his mouth pull up. He tries a bit harder. Now the corners of his eyes crinkle.

'My dear,' his wife breathes as she appears at his side. He moves his head and graces her with the same smile he had practiced for the mirror. 'You look very good. Superior. Your ideas will convince your partners, I'm certain.'

Now he smiles in earnest. How little does she know! He presses her hand softly, lifts it up to his lips, and blows a kiss on her knuckles.

The manservant accompanies him to the waiting brougham, hands him the walking stick, and says, 'I wish you a pleasant evening, sir.'

He ignores the man. The door is being closed and the horses set the carriage in motion. *Soon*, he thinks. *Soon*.

His driver stops at the marble stairs — three marble pillars carry a marble entrance. The carriage door opens; the coachman keeps his head bowed while his master alights.

He tugs at his gloves, fits them neatly in between each finger, then taps his stick on the pavement and climbs the stairs to the grand building.

A mass of people are streaming through the entrance doors, but the chatter doesn't reach his ears. He steps inside, nods at a few acquaintances while pretending to look for someone in particular. He walks to the lavatory and locks himself into one of the stalls. As soon as the first notes of *La Gioconda* trickle through the walls, he exits the building, sneaks past his waiting driver, and calls a cab. 'George Street, St Giles. Make haste!'

***

Three days have passed since her visit to Garret's abandoned room. Every afternoon now, she returns from Guy's earlier than usual, only to find St Giles a bit emptier, a bit less of a home.

She walks the streets, sometimes with Barry, sometimes alone. Often, her fruitless searches for information on Garret's whereabouts are interrupted by children with bleeding knees or infected cuts, or by adults with beaten-up faces, fractured limbs, or knife wounds.

The summer is growing hotter and germs are replicating eagerly in open wounds and on sweaty skin. All the while, the wet rattling of consumptive coughs is growing less urgent.

Tonight she walks without Barry, her feet leading her towards Clark's Mews. A string of thoughts niggle in the back of her mind. Was it pure coincidence that no one knew where Garret was and that, at the same time, the knife-man and Poppy seemed to have disappeared without a trace?

Certainly, Poppy's disappearance might be unconnected to Garret's and the knife-man's. She might have left St Giles or London all together. With a mother who had sold her to one of the most wretched brothels in the city, one can expect the girl to be street-savvy enough to survive. She must have grown up in, and hence, be used to, extreme poverty. Perhaps her mother was a prostitute, or on the brink of prostitution. That the girl is helpless, or weighed down by narrow-minded moral so as to jump off a bridge and drown herself in the river, is unlikely. But no matter how much Anna theorises, the many possibilities of Poppy's whereabouts don't narrow down to only one, don't point her to one destination, don't allow her to find the girl and learn what had happened.

For Anna, the delicate balance of her identity safely hidden in the slums, and of the constant threat to her health and wellbeing in this gritty rookery, now begin to tip towards the unfavourable. Without Garret, she feels more prone to disappear in the maze of dark alleys and filthy corners. All that's needed is a couple of newcomer garroters who don't know she's St Giles' only health insurance.

On her search for her friend, a few people told her that he might have been caught burgling. She had thought of that earlier, but found no way to prove or disprove this theory. Theoretically, she can make an enquiry at the criminal court or at the police main quarters. Practically, she can't. She has a German accent and no papers that can prove her identity. Using her male identity is out of the question. Anything connecting Dr Anton Kronberg to St Giles can eventually land her in prison. *Tomorrow*, she decides, *tomorrow I'll pay someone to go the Central Criminal Court for me*.

The disappearance of the knife-man, though, seems entirely unexplainable. But what should she do once she meets him? Politely ask him questions on Poppy's whereabouts? How laughable!

She groans and comes to a sudden halt, feeling strangely too hot. Her skin is itching, her thoughts seem sluggish.

Her gaze rests on a billboard. Her eyes don't take in the letters or the illustration. She imagines herself emerging from behind the too-small hiding place, her privates burning from overuse, a customer throwing a coin at her feet, and she picking it up eagerly. Will she end up like this, once someone discovers what she does for a living?

Anna shakes her head and rakes her fingers through her hair. Her mind has a tendency to take her onto a too-wild ride, no matter how much it reflects on reality. She wonders what's wrong with

113

her today. These useless thoughts don't get her anywhere but too close to fear and despair. Prickling runs down her body. *Might have caught the latest summer cold*, she thinks when she steps around a corner and a knife meets her throat.

'Good evening.' A whisper close to her ear. A hand curls around her elbow. She's pushed through a doorway and into a corridor. The house smells of mould and of excrements from rats and humans.

It's so dark she cannot see more than a silhouette. The man is of normal build, and a few inches taller than she. His voice is softer and higher than that of the drunkards frequenting the establishments in Clark's Mews. She detects the odour of expensive soap and the scent of virgin silk and wool — not the yarn produced by tearing up tattered remnants of clothes, then spinning the shreds to weave them into "new" fabric. The man in front of her smells of money. Lots of it.

Apparently by accident, his hand brushes over her left forearm and finds the outlines of her small jackknife. 'What is this?' he asks, his fingers probing her sleeve and extracting the tickler.

With a snort of contempt, he drops it to the ground, then slips his hand over her other arm, her stomach and waist, but no more weapons are to be found. 'I heard you are looking for me. This is most unusual, don't you think?'

She doesn't answer. Her knees and thighs are pressing together in reflex.

'I have been informed that a woman is making enquiries about me. It's usually I who chooses the women. Now it appears as though a woman picked me. I'm honoured,' he continues. The tip of his knife is resting where her pulse drums against her skin. Her lower abdomen contracts. 'But don't you think your behaviour inappropriate?'

'What?' she asks, for nothing else takes shape in her mind. She's too busy analysing as much as she can. His high, white collar shows dimly in the dark — the top hat, the light coat, the silvery glint of his walking stick's knob.

The back of his hand strikes her across her cheek. A warning that brings a sting, but is, in itself, harmless. The knife makes contact again. 'Say,' he begins and probes between her legs, 'you wouldn't be bleeding, would you?'

'I rarely do,' she answers and her silly mind begins calculating when her last menstruation was. About a year ago. She had been ill then.

'Very unfortunate.' He drops his hand and wipes it on the front of her dress. 'What do you want from me, then? You don't appear to be a prostitute. Not even a runaway girl looking for adventures with an experienced man.'

'I want to know what happened to the girl. Poppy is her name. The one whose face you cut open.'

'Of course.' He chuckles. The knife loses contact. Only a moment later, he presses it against her cheek just underneath her left eye. 'I will be patient with you and teach you a lesson. Let's call it

115

"Reality." Are you listening?' He reduces his voice to a soft whisper.

Anna breathes, 'Yes,' for nodding would drive the blade into her eye.

'Excellent. Not a single soul wishes to know what happens to whores. When they disappear, most people are grateful. Not I, mind you. But people who ask too many questions, people like you, are threatening the foundation of our modern society. Do you know why?'

'No.'

'You see, men are unable to control their animalistic urges. It is common knowledge. So what are we to do, once we are married? For the modest woman seldom desires sexual gratification. She submits to her husband for the desire of maternity and to please him. In the soul of a good woman, there is no space for sexual indulgence. She knows little of the darker, deeper desires of many a man. In order to calm man's dark side, he *must* use whores. It is in the nature of man, and that is what whores are for — to satiate. It is like everything in life. There are the ones who deserve to be served, and the ones who serve. But I wonder... Perhaps, *you* wish to satiate my animalistic urges? My control of them might be slipping any moment now.' Spite sharpens his voice, and the knife's tip is pressing hard against her skin.

'No,' croaks up Anna's throat.

'Very well, then. I trust you learnt your lesson tonight. If not, one more meeting might be

116

necessary. But it won't be as pleasant as this one. Have a good night.'

The knife disappears, and with it, the man. She slumps forward and retches. Bile hits the pavement.

Newgate

Thirty, echoes in Garret's skull. *Thirty*. The word still carries the magistrate's satisfied lilt.

He had felt very small in Old Bailey's Central Criminal Court. The charges against him were laughable. The police soon noticed that they had caught the wrong man, for he didn't look like the pickpocket they had been chasing — a skinny boy with hair as black as a raven's feathers. Yet, the police needed to catch someone, and this was Garret's misfortune.

He would have been released at once if not for the bundle of burglar equipment and the two pieces of liver stuffed with opium.

Garret had insisted that he found both at the corner of High Holborn and Broad Street. He told the magistrate how lucky he felt that the police caught him. He would have eaten the liver and would have surely died of opium poisoning. He had even folded his large hands to appear humble. But it hadn't helped much. He looked like the brute he was.

Lacking solid evidence, they couldn't detain him for very long. Owing to his build, however, his roots in St Giles, and the incriminating accessories, the magistrate decided that punishment would only do Garret good.

***

'O'Hare!' calls the warden, rattling a large ring full of keys, most of which have lost their lock long ago. Their only purpose is to impress. Here in Newgate Prison, the man with the keys is king.

Garret is led through a dingy corridor out towards the gallows. The thief holds his head high, taking in all details one last time: the moisture dripping down the vaulted ceiling, the green slime growing on cold stones, the echo of his footfall, the murmurs, shouts, and cackles of his fellow prisoners. The light at the end of the corridor is blinding, a hooded figure cuts through its centre, black on white — the executioner.

The man is holding the cat, an all-but-inviting thing. Its handle is about two feet long and shiny from regular use. The nine tails, all fourteen or fifteen inches, are twitching. He strikes at the whipping frame as though the beast needed testing. Garret knows this is done to initiate the terror. Pain comes eagerly when fear is there to welcome it.

The hangman nods at Garret and asks him to take his shirt off before he ties his hands to the wooden frame.

How considerate, thinks Garret. At least, more tears are unlikely to be added to the many his once-best shirt has already received in this godforsaken place. A week ago, he sold his jacket in exchange for food. His boots would have been next, but luckily it hadn't come to that.

The first swish bites through the air and catches on Garret's back. One drawn-out lightning of pain.

Two.

Three.

Four. His skin is growing raw, as though it's about to peel off his back. Now, the cat's tails feel more like flames than leather. She licks him again and again.

Fifteen.

Sixteen. *Ah!* Even his toes hurt with every lash. Garret clenches his teeth. *Make no sound!* he commands his throat.

Twenty-one. His lips vibrate with the grunt he cannot hold in. Every limb begins to quiver.

'Lay it on fair, will ya?' he squeezes through his teeth.

Twenty-eight.

Twenty-nine.

One more. *Ah!*

The hangman releases Garret's wrists. Steadying himself on the frame, fighting to remain upright, he squares his shoulders, nods at the man with the whip, and is escorted out of Newgate.

It takes him over an hour to reach his quarters. All the while, he swears to himself to be more careful next time. For her, at least.

Thoughts of the fragile woman, her softness when he holds her hand, her determination that could scare the devil, made his days in Newgate more bearable and harder at the same time. He was worried about her. She couldn't know where he was and she'd surely try to find Poppy and run into danger.

Two weeks in this sick place, without money to bribe the warden — all he received as food was mouldy crusts of bread. His stature protected him from violence, but every day he stood at the gates, with his hands stretched through the bars to beg for food. He often went hungry, for he didn't appear as wretched as all others. One week into prison life, he felt so weak he was not sure he could fend off the other inmates any longer.

Luck came in the shape of a pickpocket who possessed a few coins and was in need of a bodyguard. His life for Garret's, protection in exchange for food and drink. The man had already found a replacement when Garret met the cat.

The latch key scrapes through the keyhole, his hand trembles. He has nothing to drink here, not even a slice of dry bread. He drops onto the mattress with a low thud, thinking that he'll rest a little before he hunts down something to eat, and perhaps even an ale.

***

He sees her crossing the street, jumping over mule manure, the hems of her skirts dancing around her ankles. Her head tilts as she spots him. *Is it mistrust that narrows her eyes?* he wonders.

'Oy, Anna!' he calls. She stops her stride when he walks up to her.

'Hello.' She sounds as though she is disappointed to see him.

His mouth sags. 'I took a vacation.' Her left eyebrow pulls up. 'In Newgate,' he adds.

'Why?' A heavy voice, almost bored.

That she's obviously not happy to see him hurts more than his back. Her face is unusually still; no emotions flit across it.

'I'm a thief. You forgot that?'

'How come you let yourself be caught?'

'Let myself…be caught?' Garret puffs up his cheeks and looks up at the sky, searching for words in the white-and-blue. He exhales, tells his heart to shut up, turns away, and lets her stand on the pavement. He is in no mood for a sharp retort. All he wants is to go home and digest his early dinner with a good long nap.

He's barely closed the door to his room when he hears a knock. A timid one, almost apologetic. One from delicate knuckles on worn wood. He opens and sees her face. Curiously, that face looks more tired than he feels.

She tries a smile. 'I'm sorry, Garret. I wasn't very forthcoming.'

'Want a tea?'

'No. Er…yes, that would be nice, thank you.'

She snaps the door shut and leans against it. Her gaze travels through the room, now crowded with two people in it. She takes in the small straw mattress in the corner, the cupboard — stained from heavy use through generations — the one hook on the wall with a coat hanging down from it. Last time she had seen the tattered thing, it boldly told her that the thief had gone missing. Her eyes meet Garret's, who stares down at his hands.

'What is it?' she asks.

He takes up a small earthen cup and turns it for her to look inside. She steps closer. A few lonely crumbs, dried and black, dust the bottom.

'No tea.' He doesn't look up and feels ridiculously poor today.

She takes the cup, her fingers brushing his, and blows out the remains. Garret notices the dark shadows under her eyes. They make her look frail.

'The way you walked…' Anna begins. '…as though you are hurting. Did they flog you?'

He nods.

'How many strokes?' Her voice is a low caress.

'Thirty.'

Her bosom heaves once, then she's all matter-of-fact again. 'Let me take a look. It might get infected if the skin is cut.'

As he begins to unbutton his shirt, her gaze drops to her boots. Awkward silence pushes its way in. 'Anna,' he whispers. 'What happened to you? You look ill.'

She shrugs his concern off, whisks at a curl that tickles the corner of her eye.

'I missed you,' Garret mumbles, with his shirt unbuttoned, and immediately wants to slap himself.

She takes the chance to busy her hands. The gentle brush of her palm on his shoulder, lifting the cotton off his back. She handles him as though he were a butterfly. Her breath — a sharp intake, then nothing for a while before she exhales the tension.

'Do you have fresh water? And soap?' Her voice sounds constricted. Garret hasn't seen his own back and now, hearing her pain, he feels no urge to lay his eyes on it.

She picks up the jug he points to. 'It'd be better if you were to lie down,' she says, rummaging in the cupboard with her one free hand.

Garret lowers himself onto his mattress, pressing his shoulder against the wall to give her more space.

The clucking of water; the sound of soap swimming between her palms. She washes his back while he thinks of the smallness of her hands and the contrast between her body and his. *Would she let me kiss her?* he wonders. The stupid brute of a thief and the quick-witted and gentle nurse. He wishes he could shrink himself and simultaneously obtain a thorough education, all in a heartbeat.

He turns his head to look at her. A change of water, then the soap is washed off the torn skin. She dabs at it with a towel, a threadbare cotton rag, but clean enough, it appears.

'Lie down for a moment, so I can see you better,' he says softly and, he hopes, not threateningly. Then he realises how inappropriate that may have sounded. 'I didn't mean to…'

She doesn't react, only presses her palms against her eyes and mutters, 'I need to rest for a moment,' before leaning her forehead on his mattress and rolling to her side, arms wrapped around her chest.

Her face being so close to his, Garret tries to not make round eyes in wonder.

A few moments later, her mouth and brow relax with a sigh. Finally, he realises that something is wrong. He moves his arm, careful not to bump into her, and places his palm on her forehead.

The heat flicks away his own weariness. He sits up, feels her hands and her neck — all much too hot. He pulls his blanket over her, grabs the bucket, and is out on the street in a flash. Only two minutes later, he returns with fresh water and tea borrowed from a neighbour.

Standing in front of her, he feels a little helpless and shifts his weight from one foot to the other, seeking an alternative. Finding none, he pushes the blanket and her skirt up to her knees, takes off her boots, dunks two rags in the cold water and wraps them around her calves, wetting her stockings.

She moans, mutters, and falls silent again.

This he repeats every few minutes until finally, around midnight, her fever drops.

Exhausted, he lies down next to her. As his fingertips brush a curl from her cheek, thoughts of being a father and a husband put a smile on his face. He frowns and places a hand on her forehead, praying he'll wake up as soon as her fever returns.

***

Her tongue is stuck to her palate. Swallowing hurts her throat. Her eyes open and her body freezes in shock. She is sprawled across Garret's bed, his hand close to her face, his body half on the floor, half on the mattress. *How did this happen?* She searches her memories, but her brain doesn't reveal a thing. Moving a hand carefully underneath the covers, she examines her body for signs of intrusion. Her clothing clings to her skin, the stockings are moist and half pulled down, the skirts are pushed up.

Her heart hollers the song of panic; her mind can barely follow. She probes her drawers, slips a hand between her thighs. Nothing feels sore to the touch. If he had violated her, he had done it carefully. But why has she no recollections of the previous night?

Garret begins to stir and Anna decides to play dead — drops her head on the mattress and squeezes her eyes shut. She needs time to think. Her heart is knocking hard against her ribcage and she finds it hard to calm her breathing.

A whispered 'Oh!' then a gentle hand on her forehead. 'Hmm…' he says. His heavy body moves and she's about to flinch. Garret rises and walks away from her. She dares to open her eyes a fraction and sees him working at his makeshift petroleum burner.

She closes her eyes, listening to Garret's shuffling and the sound of water being poured into a pan. One part of her knows for certain that he wouldn't force himself on her. The other part keeps nagging, pushing old memories out for her to see. She flicks all fears aside to make space for facts. He could have violated her long ago, if he had wanted. It was unlikely he did so now. Why is she here? She digs in her mind, recalling that she had entered his room, that she had taken his shirt off. Images of his tortured and bleeding back hit her straight in her chest. Her eyes snap open and she shuts them again, hoping he hadn't noticed.

'Anna?' A soft voice, filled with concern.

'Garret?' She tries to cut the sound of mistrust to a minimum.

'Are you better?'

'Better? Relative to what?' She sees his confusion. 'What happened, Garret?'

'You had a very high fever. Can you not remember?' He walks up to her and drops to his knees. His hand touches her forehead again. 'It was almost gone some time past midnight. Seems it returned. You are too hot.' He walks back to his burner, the water producing little popping noises in the tin pan. Then, he clears his throat. 'I must confess something.'

She feels the heat rise in her chest, the small hairs on her arms are prickling.

'To lower your fever, I wrapped your legs in cold wet cloths. I had to… I pushed up your skirts.' He talks to the simmering water. 'And I touched your legs…rather often.'

She sees his red face, his hands holding the pot handle as though the boiling process could somehow be sped up by the pressure of his palms. It touches her heart. Her anxiety peels off and she feels ashamed for thinking the worst of him. 'Thank you.'

His face lights up. 'Want tea?'

'Yes, please.'

Her eyes linger on his busy hands and she feels herself growing calm. He sprinkles tea leaves into the boiling water, stirs them with a knife, and — as though he had a whole lot to do and no time to wait for the plant clippings to relinquish colour and aroma to the liquid — he taps the blade against the tin pan. *Tok tok tok.*

'I missed you, too,' she whispers.

Disease

'Do you need anything? Breakfast, or…something?' Garret asks, his knuckles white against the brownish cup.

'I have to leave.' She pushes up and all colour drains from her face. Her elbows quiver. With a sigh, she lays her head back onto the pillow.

'Stay,' he says softly, trying not to sound as though he's begging. His palm on her forehead feels like a cold stone too close to the fire.

'I need to send a wire,' she murmurs. 'To Guy's.'

'I can send Barry with a message.'

'No!' she cries, afraid the boy will talk about a "Miss Kronberg," which would be the end of her career. 'I'll write it. You bring it to the telegraph office. They cannot know that I live here.' A weak excuse, but good enough, it appears. Garret's raised eyebrows settle back to where they belong.

He stands up and rummages in his cupboard, swears, then returns to her side and pushes his hands under the mattress, probing left, then right. 'There it is.' He extracts a small notepad and a stump of a pencil. 'What do I write?'

'"Contracted the flu. Will send note when recovering. A. Kronberg."'

'The flu?' His hand drifts toward her forehead again, for the lack of a better idea.

She doesn't answer. Her eyes are shut, her breath shallow.

A cold shiver grips him, and he's afraid she'll die.

'Are you writing it down?' she asks and looks up at him.

Graphite whispers across paper, then he holds the note out for her to read. She nods, hoping the hospital staff will attribute the missing title to Dr Anton Kronberg being much too ill to notice.

'I have money in my room. Kitchen. Top drawer. The keys…' She fumbles in the folds of her skirts and extracts two latch keys. 'There's ointment, too. A small jar. Yellow. And buy me a few eel pies,' she says, knowing Garret must be hungry and she won't eat anything anytime soon.

'I have money,' he mutters, insulted, but she's already asleep.

***

He unlocks the door and steps inside. The smell of her room — that of soap and oiled floorboards — lets his eyes dart towards the chair he once sat upon, then to the bed he had stumbled into. Somehow, the space appears smaller now than it had been many days ago.

The mattress on the floor is a new addition. *Does she share her room with someone?* he wonders and feels the sting of jealousy.

His jaw sets in impatience. *This is not why I came,* he reminds himself, and walks to the kitchen.

A small iron stove stands there. Next to it is a wooden board atop three stacks of bricks, cluttered with a petroleum burner, a large knife and a smaller one, a mortar, cutlery stuck into in a small zinc jug, two bowls, two cups. Above these are a pan and three pots of various sizes hanging from hooks that are bound to strings and the strings bound to a sturdy stick that, in return, is fastened to the ceiling. Bundles of herbs hang from it, too.

Underneath is a bucket and a small chest of drawers. Garret opens the top drawer. He has to steady the thing while he tries to coax the drawer from its hiding place. The old wood moves with reluctance.

His fingers search through the many small items: a lone half of a pair of scissors, flax thread, wire, two screwdrivers, a pair of pliers — still intact — and several boxes and jars.

Then, Garret touches paper. He unfolds the notes and almost snatches his hand away in shock. A five pound bill, a twenty pound bill, and yet another twenty pound bill. How can she have so much money?

Behind Garret's brow, wild thoughts chase one another. What kind of criminal is Anna? She has told him she'll have to go to prison if she's caught. But caught with what? Even he — an accomplished cracksman — rarely has that much money lying around in his room.

The fact the she has more money than he spreads a very rotten feeling in his heart. He cannot support her. He cannot support a family. Garret leans on the chest of drawers and feels very unmanly. He shouldn't court her, no matter how much he likes her. *Likes*. That word doesn't describe the turmoil within. But he's not certain what love is, precisely, so he settles on *liking*. Perhaps he should not court her *because* he likes her.

He puts the notes back into the drawer, thinking that perhaps she saved money all her life. She supports neither children nor husband, and has no reasons for secret criminal activities. Ah, that husband! Garret longs to know more about her past and he wonders whether he can make her tell him her secrets, now that she has a fever.

He groans, knowing he'd never use her like that. Then his fingers touch a row of small jars. He picks one up. It's filled with a yellow paste, appearing to be the one she's asked for. He hesitates, then picks up another for safety. She is very ill; she'll surely need a lot of it.

Then he locks the door to her room and hurries to the telegraph office, telling himself that one day, she'll tell him her secrets. Perhaps not today or tomorrow, but one day she will, he is certain.

***

When he opens the door to his room, he sees the sharp contours of her shoulder and hipbone poking through his thin blanket. Her hair sticks to her head and a soft rattling issues from her throat. Her face glows with fever.

132

Garret lays his fingertips against her brow, sighs, and leaves again to get cold water from the pump. Once back at her side, he rubs her hand. 'Anna? Anna, wake up.'

Eyelids flutter. 'Hmm?'

He swallows. 'Please take off your skirts and your shirt, they are wet with sweat.'

Her fingers try to find the buttons, then give up only a moment later. He helps her, feeling more awkward than ever. The moist undergarments cannot quite conceal what lies beneath. He dunks the flannel into the bucket, careful to not gaze at the shy topography of her chest, or the dark oval where white linen hovers over her delicate navel.

The touch of cold on her arm wakes her from her stupor. 'What are you doing?'

'I'm washing you,' he simply states. 'Where do you want me to put the ointment?'

The gradual increase of consciousness seals her lips and make her eyes dart to his face and back to the bucket, the window, the kitchen cupboard. Clear thoughts are nowhere to be found.

He notices her nervousness, pulls the blanket over her shoulders, rinses the flannel, squeezes it, and offers it to her. She takes it and slips it under the covers, rubbing the stink and the sweat of disease off, while Garret rinses out the cloth, his back turned to her, his ears pricked for her huffs and moans of weakness.

'Thank you,' she whispers. 'I'll need more clean water.'

He nods and gets what she requested, again dunking the cloth into the cold water and offering it to her.

'The ointment,' she says.

He gives this to her, too, again turning away to give her a little privacy. Her hand on his back startles him.

'The ointment is for you. Help me put it on.'

He's inching away from the mattress. 'Why did you not send me to get medication for yourself?'

'There's no medication for this. Not at this stage of the disease. But your cold rags help.'

He sees the little strength bleed from her quickly, so he obeys, pulls his shirt off, and lies down next to her. Despite the warm weather, the chilly floor bites the side of his body that doesn't fit on the mattress.

The contrast of her hot fingers and the cold flannel on his lacerated back make him want to squeal like a guinea pig. She dabs at the wounds until his skin appears clean, then she spreads ointment onto each cut, crisscrossing trails of hot and cold on his back. By now, he hurts more than the previous day.

'It is a bit inflamed,' she whispers, lying down and curling her arms against her chest. 'Don't put the shirt back on. The wounds need air.' With that, she closes her eyes and exhales a long sigh.

Not good, thinks Garret, retrieves the eel pies and a jug with water, and begins to prepare tea. He's torn between hurrying up so she'll eat and drink before she falls back asleep and letting her rest a little before offering her pies and tea. His decision is made for him. Anna's face relaxes, her fists uncurl, and her breath flows quietly.

Frankenstein

'Good morning,' he says softly. 'Are you feeling better?'

She wheezes into a corner of the blanket. 'Did you sleep at all?'

He indicates the coat spread out on the ground and a shirt rolled into a pillow. 'Course I slept.' *I can sleep like this every night,* he adds silently.

She observes the nervous blinking of his forget-me-not eyes, the slight blushing of his cheeks. 'I think I'm well enough now. Would you help me get back home?'

He nods, trying to not look disappointed. 'I asked Mrs Cunningham to launder your clothes.' His hand waves towards a neat pile.

She smiles. 'Thank you.' The warmth of her voice accelerates his heartbeat.

'Do you need help to wash and…umm…probably not. I'll bring you fresh water.' He jumps up and is out the door in an instant, afraid to say something ridiculous. He always feels stupid when she's around, and he doesn't know why. She never says or does anything that should make him feel this way. And yet…

Once the bucket is filled, he stomps up the stairs, a little louder than necessary so she has ample warning. Then he knocks.

'Garret, this is *your* room. Come in!'

He steps through the door, smiling a smile that makes him feel sillier yet. He places the bucket next to the mattress, fetches a towel, a flannel, and the thin and brittle sliver of soap for her, then leaves again to buy breakfast.

He takes his time strolling down the streets, hunting for luxuries like fresh bread, butter, cheese, ham, and a bottle of milk. Anna has told him that Germans eat this stuff if they can afford it. The previous night, the two had compared their childhood breakfasts. While she'd had porridge and tea, he'd eaten potatoes with buttermilk and sheep cheese. His grandmother's stories of the Great Famine, about neighbours starving to death, and other neighbours eating rats and then dying of disease, had been repeated so often that he still knows them by heart. During the years of extreme poverty, she'd lost the ability to feel satiated. Whatever Garret's mother put on the table, it was perpetually commented on as 'Good! Good!' and devoured until the plate was so clean and shiny, one could have placed it back onto the shelve atop the scoured dishes and not have noticed a difference. As a child, Garret believed grandmother's stomach was a large barrel magically hidden in that bony body of hers, a barrel that could take in anything without ever being full.

Just as he's about to return home, he realises he has forgotten to buy milk. Garret stops and grins when an idea hits him. He'll bring Anna the freshest milk anyone can possibly get.

'Oy, Alf,' he calls through the open door of the well-known house at Drury Lane.

Harumpf, issues from the basement and a *Mooo!* follows. Clearly an invitation to approach. He climbs down the narrow staircase and a tall man slightly older than Garret sticks his head around the corner.

'Hello, Garret. The boys are about to get the manure. You want to wait?'

'No, need fresh milk for my tea now. Don't bother, Alf. I'll milk one of the ladies, you see to the boys. When are they coming?'

'Should be here any moment now. Help yourself,' Alf says and waves into the dark. 'Oh, you'll need this.'

Garret takes the offered jug and walks down to the cellar, pushes open the door that is partially blocked by manure, and steps into the dark room. Two cows are standing knee-deep in a mix of hay and shit. A square beam of light pokes through a small window just above the street; people walking through it make it flicker every so often.

Garret fetches a fork and digs a path into the manure, then bends down and touches the first cow's udder, then the other's. He decides on the animal on his right, for she appears to have more milk. He picks up the one-legged stool from a hook on the wall and ties its belt around his hip. He scoots close the cow, clamps the jug between his knees, and leans his cheek against her warm belly. Behind him, two boys begin moving manure into large baskets and hoist it up the stairs and onto the street, where a donkey cart is waiting to be filled.

Garret strokes milk from the cow's nipples, thinking of his childhood long ago. He had milked the ewes when their lambs were grown, and he'd always had the very first sip of the warm and sweet substance.

The jug is almost half-full when a high-pitched scream makes the animals jump. Garret turns his head and everything seems to slow down to a painful crawl. At first, his brain refuses to absorb what presents itself: a fork's handle is held by a trembling boy, its points impaling a wrist, a dark-purple arm peeking out from the manure.

Dream-like, Garret places the jug on a nearby shelf, extracts the fork from the boy's hand, and pulls it out of the dead flesh. He leans the fork against a wall and tries to get his bearings together. His ears sing and the world begins to wobble.

Alf and the second boy clatter through the door. 'Why are you making such a ruckus, Tom?'

Tom's mouth is sealed.

'I need a shovel.' Garret's voice is a harsh, grating noise.

'Holy…' The remainder of the sentence is stuck in Alf's throat.

'Shovel!' barks Garret, and the demanded item is slapped against his outstretched palm. Carefully, he moves the cow shit aside, feeling how the metal edge of the tool scrapes over something soft. A dirty and swollen face, throat, and chest are revealed.

139

'Alf?'

'Yes?' A quivering reply.

'Alf, I need to leave. I have never been here. Tom, fetch the coppers.' Garret looks into everyone's face and receives solemn nods in reply. He hands Alf the shovel, wipes his palms on his trousers, and takes the milk jug from the shelf. 'Tell Baylis,' he says and leaves the basement.

His legs stagger out onto the street, his eyes are blind to the passers-by. The milk suddenly seems most disgusting. Life seems most disgusting. With knees too soft, Garret's hindquarters find the next best support.

'Is that for us?' a female voice asks. Only then does he realise he's sitting in someone's home — the doorsteps of Short's Gardens' workhouse.

He nods and pushes the jug into Scotty's eager hands. The soft gulping noise wakens Betty and she demands her share. 'And the boy,' she says. 'The boy needs milk.'

The milk is gone in a heartbeat. Neither of the two old women bother to stifle their burps.

'You look ill,' observes Scotty. She pulls her waterproof closer around her bony frame and scoots forward. 'Hmm…warm milk. Never had it from over there.' She points to Drury Lane. 'Can't remember when I drank milk the last time. Didn't think it was so sweet.'

Garret doesn't reply. The wheezing of the infant in Betty's arms makes his skin crawl. He doesn't want to think of yet another death, so he stands up, but instantly retreats into the shadows of

140

the door. Two bobbies approach the house he has just evacuated.

'You found that girl,' says Scotty.

'What?'

'That girl. You found that girl,' she says loudly and slowly, perhaps thinking Garret's hearing abilities have suddenly disappeared.

He gives her a sharp look, then squeezes farther into the shadows of the doorway. 'What have you seen?'

***

Hastily, he makes his way towards home, thinking that he must tell Anna so she'll stop searching for the knife-man, but then, all of a sudden, he stumbles to a halt.

Garret gazes down at his hands, remembering the fresh bread, the ham, cheese, and butter he has left at Alf's. He can't go back there now with the coppers invading the place. With the milk in the stomachs of the two Crawler women, his hands couldn't be emptier. The other thing Garret realises is Anna's serious lack of survival instinct. He is certain she won't stop searching for the knife-man if she knows what he's done. She'll try harder.

Garret looks up at the house he lives in and — as best as he can — wipes away the images of a decomposing girl buried in cow shit.

He washes his hands and face at the nearby pump, then sets off to spend his very last coin on yet another breakfast purchase.

Walking back up to his room, his arms full and his money gone, he knows that by tomorrow, he has to solve his financial problems. Selling the jewellery from his last burglary is out of the question. His back is still hurting and the last thing he'll do is to risk being caught with expensive items a rich lady is sorely missing.

He knocks and Anna opens the door for him, her body slightly bent, her face pale with bluish shadows underneath her eyes. He helps her back to the bed, then fetches a knife and begins cutting the bread and the cheese, trying not to think of the gash in Poppy's face and that across her throat.

'Are you alright, Garret?' Anna asks.

'Tired,' he provides. 'I'm tired.'

She nods, then pours milk into the two cups and empties hers greedily.

'You must have spent a lot of money. I'd like to—' His expression cuts her off.

'I know you have more than forty pounds in your kitchen drawer. It's your money, and I don't want it.' His voice is gruff. It reminds Anna of his place and of hers. Society has determined long ago that men have the money, and women...well, whatever they have, they are supposed to share it sparingly.

'If this...' She points at the large amount of food before them. '...results in you starving or you having to go on a too-risky burglary only because you spent all your money for me, then I will not eat this.' She sets down the slice of bread and ham he's just made for her. 'I don't care who of us has fifty pounds, or a thousand, or only one shilling stashed away. But I do care whether you are happy or suffering.'

She blushes and drops her gaze.

'You buy breakfast next time,' he mumbles, stunned at her confession.

'Thank you.' She picks up her food and takes a demonstratively large bite. The cheese smells delicious, too, so she cuts off a chunk and sticks it into her mouth. 'I saw you finished *Frankenstein*.'

His head flicks towards the dog-eared book that lies half-hidden underneath his shirt-pillow. 'Hmm,' he affirms. 'You said he is the only beautiful person in this whole sad story. I don't understand this.'

'He never lied,' she provides through bits of cheese, ham, and bread.

'He murdered people who had never done him harm.' Garret bites his tongue so as not to talk about Poppy.

'Yes, he did.'

'This Elisabeth was a very nice woman. He murdered her. I see no beauty in this.'

'Hmm,' Anna says, sensing Garret's tension. 'I never thought about her much. She wasn't really there. She appeared in letters and in Frankenstein's memories, but I never saw her. Do you know what I mean?'

Garret nods. 'What about the best friend? He was murdered, too. Did he not matter, either?'

She looks up at him, startled. 'I never said that murder doesn't matter.'

143

Garret slams his buttered bread onto the cutting board and exhales a grumble. 'What was that fella's name again? That of the friend?'

'I forgot,' she answers. 'It's years ago I read the book. But there isn't much of him either. Letters, memories. The book is full with Dr Frankenstein, who talks only about himself. I believe the word used most often is "I."'

Garret's fists lose their tension. 'Yes, he's quite the wimp. Always suffers from all kinds of…what's it called? Nervous inflictions?'

'Afflictions, yes.' She smiles at him. 'You didn't like him?'

'Of course I didn't! He is…don't know.'

'Full of self-pity?'

'Yes. And he keeps saying he would die to save his friend's life or his wife's. But I can't believe it.'

Feeling proud of Garret in an odd way, Anna says, 'I guess he believed himself heroic when he said things like "I would die to bring her back," or whatever it was he said. The more I read, the more I disliked him. He talks about love and loss, but doesn't seem to know what it means to love and to lose someone.'

'But only because that man is an idiot, doesn't make the other beautiful!'

She sets her cup down and rests her head on the pillow. 'I'm sorry. I'm making you angry.'

Garret's posture slumps a little. 'You don't make me angry.'

144

She pats the side of the mattress. 'Sit, and I'll try to explain myself.'

He does as she told him, and she takes his hand into hers. 'Frankenstein made a feeling, thinking human being. One he discarded as soon as it twitched to life. He made a body and murdered a soul. He did not think of loving and losing when he made the creature, he only wished to know whether was possible. He thinks only of himself and the greatness he could accomplish. But he doesn't know where true greatness lies, because he was never humble enough to see it. I believe that the creature's appearance resembled his creator's soul. A large and artificial puzzle of things that seemed useful when examined out of context, but monstrous and ugly when put together. But the creature was, in fact, beautiful. The blind man saw him for what he was. He communicated as clearly as he could; he was gentle, he sought love, and he asked for knowledge.'

Garret feels compelled to remind her. 'He is a murderer.'

'Ah, yes. And this is where it gets complicated. Does he belong to our species? He has been created by a man who used pieces of men, so the creature can be categorised as human. But then, he's not recognised as a member of our species; his creator rejects him, calls him a monster, and every human being he meets — every human who sees his outer shell, his appearance, I should say — runs away screaming. So if he's not human, can he be a murderer? You said he is a murderer, but then you are, too. Think of all the pork pies you have eaten. But if he is human, then we could indeed call him a murderer, but are we allowed to do this without blaming his creator and ourselves for all this violence? Frankenstein made him, and then he took everything away from him. He didn't show him what compassion is, he didn't show him how precious life is. None of us humans did. What follows is violence, a natural reaction to mental and emotional torture.'

Garret nods slowly, then shakes his head. 'You cannot believe the monster was justified in murdering these people!'

'I didn't say that. I said that he was the most beautiful person in this whole sad story. But I should be more specific. There were two main characters, Frankenstein and his monster. And I definitely prefer the company of the monster. Even after he had killed.' She brushes breadcrumbs from the blanket.

'I cannot believe you find a murderer *beautiful*.' Now Garret has no doubt that telling Anna about Poppy's body would be a very bad idea indeed.

'I know,' she says and closes her eyes. 'But a murderer is also always a human being. He always has a soul.' She sighs. 'I'm tired. Let me rest for a little before I leave.'

'You don't have to leave,' he whispers.

'I do. You know…' She yawns.

'Yes?'

'Most of the time, I don't like humans. They could all be apes; it wouldn't make too much of a difference to me.'

Garret's breath stalls. His mind refuses to provide a meaningful analysis of Anna's statements. 'I don't believe you. You help people every day. You wouldn't do it if you didn't like them at all.'

Several moments pass without a reply. Her breathing has grown deeper and slower, and he believes she has fallen asleep.

But then she stirs a little. 'Because when people are sick and weak, when they fear death, they reveal who they are. They wear no masks and I can see their souls.'

'Do you like them, then?'

She sighs again, and searches for his hand that had withdrawn a moment earlier. 'Souls are always beautiful. But you…' She presses the back of his hand against her forehead. '…have an exceptionally beautiful soul.'

The pressure of her fingers around his slackens and she falls into her first restful and deep sleep for days.

Baylis

Baylis' apron is, as usual, marked by a long day's work. The man seems to be everywhere at once. In the kitchen, stirring two enormous vats of soup made of whatever ingredients he can find, or at the counter talking to Ramo Sammy who, now one-toothed, spends most of his days here, sitting and slurping what Baylis pours into his bowl. When Baylis isn't to be found at any of the aforementioned locations, he'll most likely be standing at the entrance door to his shop, with one hand leaning against the frame and his sharp gaze sweeping over each and every street arab lined up to obtain enormous helps of pudding for a halfpenny. He's always a little surprised by the trust they give him, despite him having worked as a plainclothes detective for more than seven years.

Now, all street arabs are gone and Ramo is dozing in a far corner of the shop, next to the kitchen door where he's not in anyone's way.

When Garret sneaks in through the back, Baylis locks up and closes all shutters.

A group of men are already sitting at the largest table, their faces solemn. 'We will discuss this in a quiet manner,' Baylis begins. 'Every man shall speak his mind. There'll be no shouting, and no interrupting each other. I believe it is Garret who met the girl in question before she was murdered?'

148

Murmur spreads at the word *murdered*. Baylis bangs his flat hand upon the tabletop. Silence settles at once.

Garret clears his throat. 'No, never met her. But Anna...the nurse. You know the nurse, don't you?' He looks at everyone and all heads are bobbing in reply. 'She treated the girl's injuries.'

'Do you know what injuries precisely?' Baylis asks.

'Anna told me the girl's mouth had been...cut open. Her cheek.' Garret traces his fingers across his face, then taps them onto the polished wood. 'I heard from others that he likes to run his knife over women's skin.'

The men are nodding. 'I heard that, too!' issues from every mouth.

'Anything else?'

'I talked to Rose at Fat Annie's, but she doesn't know much. Poppy was sold by her mother. Her last name was...umm. I forgot.'

'You asked Rose about Poppy?' one of the Worthing twins interrupts.

Garret groans. 'Anna asked me to talk to her. She wanted to know why Poppy disappeared, and who that man is.'

More muttering fills the room, showing discontent.

'Quiet, now,' warns Baylis. 'What the woman does is her business.'

'I saw the girl's face, too,' the older Worthing twin supplies.

'Me, too,' his brother says, and continues, 'Our sister talked to us. She suggested the girl could live in Alf's attic, and...' His face falls into his hands. His brother claps him on his shoulder. Baylis waits while the others shuffle their feet. 'She thinks it's her fault the knife-man killed her.'

'Bollocks!' Nate barks and drives the tip of his penknife into the table.

'I need that table, Nate.' Baylis gives the old man a warning stare. 'I heard Poppy was dismissed from Fat Annie's because of the wound the man inflicted. Is that true?'

'Yes,' says Garret. 'That's what Rose said.'

'She's bad for the business. Fat Annie, who is. Squeezes the last bit of sanity from her girls. That woman needs a good spanking, that's what she needs.' Nate's knife hovers over the kinked wood, a grumble from Baylis' throat makes him lay it flat onto the table. 'Butcher didn't protect her. Now look at this mess!' Nate crosses his arms over his chest. 'He should be here, too. Butcher, I mean.'

'Butcher! Wouldn't let *that* man into my house even in bright daylight!' shoots from the older Worthing's mouth.

'Quiet, now!' warns Baylis. 'Hot blood gets us nowhere. Has anyone seen the knife-man, and if so, when and where? Does this man even have a name? And for your information — that he pulled a knife through Poppy's face doesn't mean he pulled it through her throat.'

Protests erupt from all mouths, Baylis whacks his hand upon the tabletop again. When Garret says, 'But it does,' silence falls.

'Have you seen him?'

'No, I haven't. But about two weeks ago, one of the women living on the workhouse's stairs — Scotty's her name — had seen him and Poppy enter the house. That same house the girl lived in. That same house we found her buried in cow shit.'

'It might be strong evidence, but it's no proof,' Baylis points out.

'He was seen pushing the nurse into one of the houses at Clark's Buildings,' mutters Nate.

'What?!' barks Garret and jumps up, his chair falling onto its back with a loud clatter.

'I need that chair, too,' huffs Baylis, but his protest is ignored by everyone in the room.

'One of our girls saw it. Didn't think much of it at first, for he's known to pay well for a few scratch marks. Took her a while to remember that Anna is no strumpet. She said she saw him pocket his knife when he walked out onto the street. She said that he looked satisfied.' Nate shakes his head in disbelief at so much stupidity. 'She isn't the brightest,' he says with a shrug.

Baylis's worried gaze is attached to Garret's fingers clawing the tabletop's edge. 'Has anyone seen him recently?'

All men shake their heads.

'Ask Butcher.'

'I'll talk to him,' Garret rasps. No one objects.

151

'What did the bobbies say? Did the body look as if she had been killed and buried two weeks ago?' asks Baylis.

The colour drains from Alf's face. 'I've never before seen a corpse in cow manure. Can't tell if it had been there for two weeks. But it surely looked...ripe.'

'When did you clean up last?'

'Umm.' Alf scratches his chin and looks up at Baylis. 'Might have been two or three weeks. My missus was ill and...' He waves the last words away as though they were blowflies.

'Her skin was blue and red, marbled, some parts were black,' whispers Garret. 'Her stomach was bloated, the cuts across her cheek and her throat were black gashes. Her eyes...I'll never forget this. Maggots and beetles everywhere. Crawling out of her mouth, eyes, wounds.'

Hands clap over mouths and eyes. Someone burps, followed by an audible swallow of bile. Only Nate just sits there, his jaws working, his expression empty as though he isn't present.

Baylis exhales a growl. 'What about the police, Alf?'

'What do you expect? Two bobbies puked into my basement, then left the house. Stood at the side of the street, waited for an inspector who didn't come, all the while joking about runaway girls. I asked, "Have you not seen the gash across her throat?" They said they didn't look that closely, given the state the body was in and all. I asked, "Have you not seen that the girl was murdered?"

and they told me to clean up the basement, because it is illegal to keep cows down there.'

Baylis throws up his hands. 'Goddammit! And what happened to the body?'

'Men from the morgue came and took her. The inspector arrived two hours later and threw a fit because the body was gone, the manure was gone, and the cows confiscated. My cows gone…' mutters Alf. 'I don't know what I'll do now without my girls.'

Baylis pushes his hands into his trouser pockets and begins pacing the room. Everyone is waiting for him to open his mouth. He does so more than fifteen minutes later.

'You all know I worked for the police. What I'll tell you now is only my opinion. I could pay a visit to the Bow Street Police Station and inquire about the body and any progress made in the case, should there be a case at all. However, all evidence has already been destroyed and the body was in an advanced state of decomposition. I doubt very much my questions will result in helpful answers. I believe the police will never find the girl's murderer; I doubt they'll start looking. That the knife-man did this is very likely, but we don't know for certain.' He turns to face the group of silent men. 'If I were to go to the police and show interest in this case, and then — hypothetically speaking — *something* happens to the knife-man and the police hear about it, they'll know where to look first.'

'The man must disappear,' says Garret, who is the first to grasp the meaning of Baylis' words.

'I agree. But...' Baylis holds up his hand. '...we did not prove him guilty. Keep this in mind. He can be as innocent as my daughter, or as innocent as yours.' He points at Nate.

'What I know is this,' Garret begins. 'A very dangerous man who might or might not be a murderer, threatened the life of the only woman who bothers saving our sorry behinds should they ever get infected or injured. The only one with medical skills and no interest in charging money, I should say. If she's gone...' The large man swallows, his eyebrows pushing together.

'What can we do?' asks the younger Worthing brother, rage in his eyes and a freshly pulled-out knife in his hand.

'What *you* can do?' says Baylis, counting a total of four knifes on the table. 'Use your brains before you use your weapons! Talk to Butcher. We'll meet again tomorrow night.'

Garret pushes away from the table. He stares at Nate, Alf, the Worthing twins, and Baylis. A silent agreement settles, making the air in the room heavy and the hearts of the men rumble.

Alf

He stands in his basement, taking in the emptiness of the room and the lack of farm odour. He misses the soft breathing, the swishing of tails, and gentle mooing of his two girls.

The emptiness occupies the corner of his vision, while its centre is too crowded — crowded with a memory he cannot blink away.

'Alf?' issues from the corridor above. 'Where are you, you useless piece of crap? Get your hindquarters up here. The dustmen are coming any minute now. You want me to carry this all by myself? Alf!'

The man turns to climb the stairs. His posture is slightly more crooked than it was just a moment ago. 'I'm coming, Beth, my dear.'

'You have that look upon your face again,' she says while both drag out a large bucket full of ashes, a pile of potato peels now rotten, a tattered sack of unknown origin, and a shovel full of faeces from the cat. 'I'll be damned, Alf. That little whore got your head messed up.'

'I don't like it when you call her that.'

'But she was a whore, wasn't she? I'm glad she's good and done with. Might have lured you into her bed one fine day. God knows what—' She catches herself and throws a sharp glance at her husband. 'If she hadn't already.'

'No one lures me into bed but you, Beth,' Alf says softly. But he doesn't look at her, which goes

155

unnoticed by his wife, for she's busy searching the street for the dustmen. And there they come, one tired old donkey followed by a decrepit cart upon which sit two men wearing the dirtiest clothes in the whole of the British Empire.

'Them extra ones,' she mutters, meaning that this pair is not the government-appointed, but the fake version. It doesn't make too big of a difference to her, but it does so to the rest of the city — these two men will pick up the refuse and charge a fee, just like proper dustmen do. However, their load will never arrive in the central dust-yards; instead, it will be dumped on some unlucky street far away from here.

Once the coin is exchanged for refuse and wheels clatter across cobbled streets, Alf takes care to be more attentive. He opens the door for his wife and asks when lunch will be ready. As soon as he hears her bang pots about in the kitchen, he creeps up the stairs, higher and higher, until he reaches the attic.

The door creaks open and pigeons flutter through a hatch. Dust swirls though milky daylight. In a far corner, a lonely pile of straw and a blanket indicate the one missing inhabitant who hadn't had a chance to pack her belongings. The other boarders left the day Poppy's body was found.

Alf steps forward, feeling as though something or somebody pulls him toward the bedding. He remembers the last time he felt this pull. It had come from a friendly young woman, whose mouth had no harsh words for him. His knees had hurt a little when he knelt down next to her, here on these floorboards, when everyone else was out and about to attend to whatever daily businesses they had to attend to. His scrubby cheeks and chin must have hurt her wound a little, for she flinched when he kissed her. All he longed for was a little affection. After all, it was her trade.

'Alf, get your wrinkled behind into the kitchen! Your stew is getting cold and I'm certainly not warming it up a fourth time!'

Alf sighs, tips his fingers at the two brown specks on the floor. 'Odd,' he whispers. He spits on a corner of his sleeve and wipes them off the kinked wood.

Nate

He's haggling with a costermonger, pointing at cabbages, cucumbers, carrots, and a basket of eggs when a familiar face shows in the crowd.

'Anna!' he calls, waves his arm and holds up an index finger, then turns to pack his purchases onto a small cart. Once everything is secured, he turns to find her in the mass of people, but she's already at his side and offers to pull his load. Although forthcoming, the gesture insults him. He shakes her off with a gruff, 'Don't be ridiculous, girl!'

When he begins to walk, the four wooden cart wheels jiggle across the coarse cobblestones, threatening to jump off their pivots. His stick, however, always finds the very top of each stone, never slipping into the cracks to get stuck, never making him stumble.

'Is your leg hurting?' she asks.

'No, this's not what I want to tell you. Say, are you still looking for Poppy?' He tries to give his voice the naive undertone of an old man with little brainpower.

She almost jumps in surprise. 'Do you know where she is?'

'No, but I heard from…someone that you've met the fella in question. The one with the knife.'

'I did,' she says.

From the corner of his vision, he sees her pressing a fist against the pit of her stomach, and he feels a sudden urge to grab her by her shoulders, shake her, and shout, 'Do you know how lucky you are?' But he does no such thing.

'When I was a young man, I was a soldier and saw more death than anyone should ever see in his life. And I took lives. I saw men with very dark souls. Very dark. Can't tell if they even had one.'

He blinks and his gaze grows distant, flitting over people, their wares and faces, and farther up to houses, windows, roofs, and finally, the cloud-covered sky. But his mind doesn't see what his eyes see. His mind races across battlefields, over corpses of hundreds of men, failing to understand why people believe war is a heroic thing.

Gradually, the clanking of sabres and cracking of shots is replaced by rattling of wheels. He recalls he has an audience. Gazing at her, he says, 'I can see it in a man's eyes if he's a murderer — if he enjoys it. You know what I mean?'

She nods at her shoes. 'I think so.'

'The man you are looking for is such a man. That's why I never let him into our boarding house. Once, he offered ten times the usual fee. I showed him my service revolver, pressed it against his unblemished upper-class nose. Haven't seen him since.'

'How can a well-to-do man enter St Giles without getting mugged?'

'Cabs drop 'em off at Clark's Buildings; everyone knows they bring business. No one will steal from a man who comes to bring in money.'

159

'Does that happen often?' she asks, wondering why she hadn't noticed the import of wealthy customers to filthy establishments.

Nate shakes his head. 'No, not often. Only few of the rich have that *taste...*' He comes to a halt, his cart ceasing the noise. He clears his throat and scratches his chin, hoping he looks and sounds reluctant to share information.

'I hear things,' he begins. 'From the girls. Some is codswallop, some the truth. They say Poppy worked the street for a few nights, and slept in the attic of the house at Drury Lane where the two cows are kept in the basement. The ones that one can milk for a fee. Nice white-and-brown ones. You know those?' He sees Anna's perplexed stare and wonders if she believes his charade of muddle-headedness. 'Oh, yes. Poppy. One night, she meets that man. I don't know who saw it and how many mouths have added to the story. But this much is true: the two entered the house she lives in, and that was the last time anyone saw the girl.'

'Did you summon the police?'

He snorts. 'What for?'

The cart is set in motion again and Nate shuffles along. At times, such as today, he feels three-legged, with his stick supporting much of his weight. He senses her analytic stare, giving him a prickling in his neck.

He stops once more and turns to her. 'Listen to me, Anna. When a rich man injures a St Giles prostitute, what do you believe will happen?'

'Nothing?'

160

'Precisely. The police will do nothing because, in their eyes, we are all criminals. No one will investigate…' He cuts himself off.

'Investigate?'

He hears suspicion in every breath she takes. 'She was injured and she disappeared. No one will investigate this, and certainly not *here*. You seek justice where none is to be found.'

'Don't you have your own sense of justice?'

'Of course I do. Why else would I protect my girls from men like him? He isn't the first, and certainly won't be the last. But I'm not egoistic enough to chase after him.'

'Why would that be egoistic? You would prevent—'

'Goddammit, you are naive!' Nate searches for words. Impatiently, he sets the pull-handle of his cart onto the road. 'If I left Mum's boarding house to run around and find all monsters who fancy sticking knifes into girls, I'd certainly be somewhat of a hero, even if I got myself killed in the process. Meanwhile, Mum and the girls are unprotected, no one cooks for them, no one lends them an ear when they need one. And they certainly do need that often! It is a small role I'm playing, but it's my role, and I'm proud of it. You, on the other hand…' He pokes his gnarled finger against her forehead. 'If you go out to find that fella and get yourself gutted, then you are responsible for all your neighbours dying of injuries and disease because you are not here to care for them. Quite idiotic, if you ask me.'

161

He sees her wide-eyed stare and knows she analyses every word he says and every bit of information she suspects him to withhold.

'Nate?' she says with an audible clump in her airways. 'Why is Mum called Mum?'

'Because she opened the boarding house together with our daughter.' He clears his throat. 'I learned about the child only a few years later.'

'Your…' He sees her searching her memories for all the faces of women she'd treated, but she doesn't seem to find one who looks remotely like Nate or Mum.

'Who is she?'

'Our daughter? Long gone. Long gone.' A tired mutter, one that opens all senses wide if one only knows how to listen.

'Why do you keep this boarding house?' she says hoarsely.

'It's all she has.'

She wants to ask more questions, but all of them will hurt, so she keeps her mouth shut.

'I told your friend to keep an eye on you.'

'What friend?' she asks, but already knows the answer.

Butcher

He stares down at his fingers. The nails need a trim. But at least they are clean. Eight years ago, if he remembers correctly, a perpetual brown rim stained his fingernails and the cracks surrounding them. Brown were the fine furrows snaking around one another, forming weird pattern on the pads of his fingers. Brown was the base of each and every hair growing on the backs of his hands and his lower arms. He had been elbow-deep in blood and guts of swine and cattle, a whole of ten hours each day. He'd turned deaf for the screaming of animals, the buzzing of flies, the sounds of knifes and saws and hammers, but the blood on his skin, the colour of it, and the odour, all of which accompanied him wherever he went, had bothered him deeply.

Now, it's the grunts of satisfied men, or the grunts of unsatisfied ones, and the fake outcries of pleasure from the girls' mouths he's learned to ignore. When Mr Steward stuck his knife into the new girl's face, he'd ignored her cry, too. Hadn't expected anything else from a girl that young and inexperienced. They all needed breaking in, and he is glad he hadn't done it on this one.

Some pimps fancy doing it, but for Butcher's taste, the sounds the girls make are often too close to the squealing of a butchered pig. Yet, not close enough to push the noise into the deaf corner of his mind. So he tries to stay away from the breaking-in business. Other than that, he doesn't mind the girls'

163

favours in exchange for delaying the rental payments for a day or two.

Butcher hears a heavy knock on the brothel's front door, and he's a bit puzzled. The afternoon is still so young; the whores have barely prepared their rooms. He opens the door and takes a step back. 'Your prick must be itching badly,' he grunts at Garret. 'Rose isn't ready. None of the—'

'We need to talk,' interrupts Garret and pushes into the corridor. 'Is anyone in the kitchen?'

'What do you want?' Suspicion makes Butcher's voice harsher than usual. He isn't accustomed to anyone reaching eye level with him. He could deal with a tall stick of a man, but having to look up at a man of his own build and half an inch more height is more than irritating.

'Poppy is dead. I want to talk with you about the man who cut her face. Now, get into the kitchen. I don't want the whole neighbourhood to hear what I have to say.'

Reluctantly, Butcher moves his feet towards the back of the house. He toes the kitchen door open, shoos two women out of the room as though they are a pair of sparrows, then positions himself behind the table, arms crossed, face stern. 'How do you know the girl's dead?'

'Found her in a pile of cow shit. When have you last seen the man?'

'Might have been a week ago.'

'Was it a week ago or was it not a week ago?'

Butcher watches Garret's hands ball to fists and press onto the tabletop. Knuckles whiten, blood vessels bulge underneath yellow fuzz. 'Pretty sure a week.'

'Will he come back?'

'Don't know why he wouldn't.'

'Who's serving him?' Garret's question come as quick and as sharp as gun fire.

'Whoever has her monthly thing.'

'Menstruation. It's called menstruation. You work in a brothel and can't even say menstruation. Can you say quim?'

Now Butcher's fists press onto the tabletop, too. The pair appears like two bulls getting ready for a furniture-shattering brawl.

'Quim,' says Butcher.

Garret can't hold in a snicker, although he knows it might tip the other man over the edge.

Butcher slams his knuckles onto the wood and barks a laugh. 'The man's name is Steward. Not his real name, mind you. But unusual enough for a customer. The others are all Smiths, Williams, Millers, and Whites.' He waves at Garret, then grows solemn. 'So you believe he killed that girl?'

'Yes.'

Butcher pulls back a chair and sits down. Garret does the same.

'What is your plan?'

Garret takes a deep breath and says calmly, 'My business. All I want from you is to send a boy to my room when *Mr Steward* comes to visit.'

Butcher chews a piece of callus off the side of his finger, spits it onto the floor, and nods. 'He's a cunning fella. Have you ever seen his face?'

Garret shakes his head.

'Did any of the others?'

Garret's stiff expression tells Butcher there are indeed other men involved.

'What's up with his face?' asks Garret.

'Nothing in particular. Just saying that he'll know something's up when he sees a familiar face on a man following him. Nate's for example. Or mine.'

'No worries,' says Garret and pushes away from the table. He has the feeling he has said too much already.

The Longest Knife

She lets a handful of green coffee beans fall slowly into the pan. *Clink clink clink* they sing when they hit the heavy cast iron. The fire is hot and soon the beans begin to crackle and pop, releasing a sharp, yet mouth-watering aroma.

She tosses the beans and swirls them in the pan until their colour reaches a brown so dark it's dangerously close to black. She blows at the loose skins and they fly in all directions. With the coffee oil coating their outsides and the skins gone, the beans are shiny and clean and beckon to be touched and smelled. She bends down and inhales their rich scent, then pours them into the mill and sits down on her chair.

The mill clamped between her knees, her legs wobble with each turn of the crank. The aroma intensifies and reaches a new high when she pulls out the small drawer at the bottom and holds the powder up to her nose.

She pours the ground coffee into a pot, adds water, and sets it on the stove. Her eyes are transfixed by the murky liquid. It boils up once, is then taken off the stove for the foam to settle, and placed over the fire yet again. She does this three times, while her mind is empty save for the few thoughts on the procedure at hand.

She lets the coffee settle in the pot, then she pours herself a cup, sits down at her table, takes a first sip, and lets her mind pick apart all that she'd learned.

Nate gave her information today, but also withheld information. His intention was clear — to keep her away from the knife-man, surely to protect her.

The few people who know she tried to find Poppy are Butcher, Rose, Sally, Barry, and Garret. The last time she mentioned the girl's name is at least two weeks ago. What caused Nate to approach her today? Why didn't he say a word when she performed the abortions at Mum's?

His reaction to this whole affair was most unusual. Rarely does he talk that much. He stated that *someone* told him she'd met the knife-man. But why would anyone find it noteworthy enough to tell *him?* Except, of course, if one of his girls had seen it. But how would he know she was looking for that man? A simple guess, perhaps?

The only person who knew she was looking not only for Poppy, but also for the knife-man, was Garret. Would Garret tell Nate? And if so, why?

Garret had seen Rose and asked her questions on Poppy's whereabouts. Ah! Garret had asked about the knife-man, too. But the women of Fat Annie's didn't talk much with the ones working at Mum's, as far as Anna knew. Why would Rose tell anyone that Garret had inquired about the knife-man? Besides, back then, no one could have guessed a connection between Anna and Garret. Later, yes. Now, the two are seen walking together rather often.

Anna frowns. Too many strands of possibilities are tangling her mind. She needs to take another step back.

She stands, brushes back her hair with her fingers, inhales deeply, and walks up to the window.

A simple guess, a suspicion, made Nate come out of his oyster shell, out of his I-speak-only-three-word-sentences routine. Is this likely?

She shakes her head. Much likelier is that Nate knows what Garret knows. Wouldn't it make sense then that Garret knows what Nate knows, too — that Poppy lived and disappeared at Drury Lane? Yet, Garret never mentioned it. Why?

Anna takes a good long sip from her coffee and looks down onto the dark street. Shadows of people are moving about. *The silence,* she thinks. *The silence speaks the loudest.*

She sets the cup down. Nate told her about his past, he even talked about his lost daughter. Not once did she hear him give anyone the smallest bit of personal information. Every word he'd told her said only one thing — *do not get near the knife-man!* This allowed only one conclusion — Nate is terrified.

But what scares him so? What happened at Drury Lane? Garret and Nate seem to know details that shock both enough to try to shield her. Garret had been worried about her before. But so far, he had not tried to stop her. He had even helped obtain information. All there is now, is a wall of silence, and something must be brewing behind it.

169

'Very well, then,' she says aloud and decides to pay Poppy's attic at Drury Lane a visit, but not before observing Fat Annie's for a little while to see if Butcher was involved somehow. After all, he didn't intervene when Poppy was injured. She hopes he has a hand in this, for it will surely be easier to press information from a man as dull as him. The overprotective Garret and the extra-wise Nate have obviously decided that she's too delicate to know a thing.

***

Anna locks the door to her room. Her knees feel a little softer than usual, her heart rumbles faster, her hands are clammy. The long knife she keeps in her kitchen drawer is now tied to her thigh and reachable through a cut in her skirts. She has practiced slipping her hand through the opening she made and extracting the weapon without its handle catching on the fabric. In and out, out and in; it took approximately half a second from lowering her hand to pulling the knife through the slit.

Her teeth find her cheek and she bites down on the soft flesh to stop herself from trembling. Then she steps out onto the street and turns towards Clark's Mews.

When she's passing Fat Annie's, Butcher gifts her a friendly smile. *As suspected*, she thinks, crinkling her brow. A few more steps, then she reaches her destination and slips into the shadows.

It's the same corridor she was pushed into. The same creaky door, the same scrunching underneath her soles. Only the odours of expensive soap, wool, and silk are lacking. Fat Annie's — just across the street — is in full view. Anna opens her senses wide.

She doesn't have to wait long. Her breath hurts in her throat when she sees Garret stepping out of the brothel.

She tells herself to stay put. She tells herself that he is not why she had come here. And yet, the mix of anxiety that he might get hurt and frustration that he didn't think her trustworthy enough makes her jaw clench.

All of a sudden, Butcher is pointing in her direction, and Garret is racing faster than she'd ever expect of a man his build. She takes a step back, pushing farther into the dark just before the rotten door slams against the corridor wall.

'Come out at once so I can give ya a good spankin'!'

She doesn't reply, so he steps through the door and grabs her arm.

'Sod off, Garret!' She kicks at his shin.

'What's that? A fly fart?'

He doesn't let go of her arm, so she kicks again and again, making him more furious yet. He wraps an arm around her and hoists her onto his shoulder.

'What the blazes? Put me down! Put me down, for Christ's sake!' Her knees push against his

171

chest without effect, her fists pummelling his back seem to leave him untroubled.

'Wha' the dickens's *tha'?*' he exclaims when something sharp pokes the bend of his elbow. He fumbles through the layers of her skirt, perfectly aware of how inappropriate that is, and extracts a long knife. Shock holds his tongue for a moment, then he chucks the weapon towards Butcher and calls, 'Keep that for me, will ya?'

He stomps along Church Lane, muttering, 'Dammit, woman!' and not listening to her protests at all. When she grows silent, he asks, 'Are you alright?'

She doesn't answer.

'Well,' he says. 'Is alright if ya hate me, as long as ya don't get yerself killed.'

'Put me down, Garret,' she says hoarsely.

The resigned tone makes him stumble. He has never heard her speak like this. 'I'll bring you home first, so you can't run away before I get to say my part.'

She hides her face in her hand, for she doesn't want to see the giggling and pointing neighbours. They must all believe that Garret is finally taking his pigheaded girlfriend to bed.

He forces the lock of the door to her house, then the one to her room. Once inside, he sets her onto her feet. 'Sit,' he commands and points to a chair.

She walks to the window instead and leans her forehead against the glass.

172

'Anna,' he pleads, pushing the door shut. 'Look at me.'

She rubs the moisture from her eyes and turns to face him.

'*What* did you plan to do?' he asks.

'What happened at Drury Lane? What do you, Butcher, and Nate know?'

'Why the knife?' It takes Garret a moment to realise that she knows more than she should.

'Just in case…'

'Just in case?' Garret's eyebrows reach a mocking angle, but he calls them to order soon enough. 'I simply grabbed you, Anna. You didn't reach for your knife, because you wouldn't stab *me*. But I swear, your kicks and punches did nothing to me. You'll need more force to run a knife through a grown man. I thought *you*, with all that medical knowledge, should know this. That fella might be smaller than me, but he can surely hurt you bad. Either he does it in some dark alley where no one can see you and no one can help you, or he simply walks into your room. The lock here…' He points behind him. '…is so weak I only *leaned* against it to open it! It didn't even make much noise. The same crap is installed down there.' He waves towards the entrance door to the house.

Her jaws are working and she knows that he's correct. 'There is one thing that hurts more than anything else,' she whispers. 'Helplessness. I feel like dying when I'm helpless.' She looks up at him. 'Never do this again.'

173

She sees his face gaining the colour of a very ripe tomato. 'I know you helped me, Garret. I know you want to protect me. By tomorrow, I'll forget how it felt to be dragged away against my will, because you did it not for yourself, but for me. But this man…If I don't do anything, I'm helpless.'

'And what am I then? An idiot? Are you the only one who cares? Don't you think it's insulting? Do not treat me like a bystander. I do have my pride.'

She sees the bulging blood vessels on his temples and decides to be quiet for a moment.

'I talked with Butcher and Fat Annie tonight,' he says. 'That man will never again enter St Giles.'

'What are you planning?'

He snorts and crosses his arms over his chest. 'You have so many secrets, Anna. This one will be mine.'

She frowns, and Garret's patience fails him yet again. 'Should I see you at Clark's before I tell you it's safe to go there, I'll drag you away just as I did today. And this time, I *will* give you a spanking!'

He rubs his scalp and his lightning-struck mop of orange hair is sticking out every which way. She suppresses a smile, knowing he'd never even hurt a fly.

'I promise I'll stay away,' she says, and means it. There are other ways to obtain information.

The Lion

He paces along the wall, past the window and back, again and again. His eyes don't register what's on the other side of his pupils. A decomposing body is burned on his retinae. When a knock disturbs his restlessness walking, his heart stumbles. He opens the door and looks down at a boy of probably eight years of age.

'Sixpence first, information second,' the boy says and holds out his left palm.

'Butcher gave it to you already,' Garret grumbles in warning.

The small hand hides in a patched-up trouser's pocket. 'Balls,' mutters the boy. 'Butcher said it's time. He didn't say what time, though. But the church bells—'

'Nothing to do with *that* time, Will,' interrupts Garret and fetches a bundle from the mattress. 'You go home now. Oh! Wait. You can earn another sixpence.'

The boy, Will, grins and holds out his hand once more. Garret fumbles through his pockets and extracts a coin. 'Keep an eye on the nurse for me tonight. And that boy she's dragging around. Barry is his name. Make sure they stay far away from Clark's, and take care they don't spot you.'

'Done,' Will says, hides the coin in his fist, and dashes off.

***

Garret waits, protected by darkness and a sheet of rain. He feels as though his rage makes him glow bright scarlet. His hand begins to hurt, so he slackens his iron grip on the mallet. Deep breath in, deep breath out. It won't help to lose reason before the time has come.

Yet, he cannot wipe away the images of a sharp blade pressing against Anna's throat. Not knowing what had happened in the dark, his imagination wants to go rampant. He cannot fathom why Anna never told him about it and why she never asked for help. Real help. Not that visit to the brothel the other night. She won't even tell him when she's scared or hurt or in danger! What's wrong with this woman?

Garret growls, then pulls himself together and focusses his attention back to Fat Annie's. *Perhaps I'm not trustworthy,* he thinks. The mallet in his hand agrees, as does the clasp-knife in his breast pocket.

The brothel door opens and light pours onto the wet pavement. A well-dressed man steps out, opens his umbrella, and turns down Clark's Buildings. Garret locks eyes with Butcher, who gives him a small and affirmative nod in return.

Garret hurriedly sets his feet in motion, pressing his body into every shadow large enough to hide his bulk.

The man turns onto High Street, then onto Arthur Street. He doesn't seem to notice the large cart blocking the view to New Oxford Street, with its many omnibuses, cabs, and people. The three men smoking next to the vehicle go unnoticed as well.

In a moment, it will be too late. Garret's mind shows him Drury Lane, the knee-deep cow manure with a girl's bloated body half buried in it, the maggots, the gashes. When the dead girl's face begins to look too much like Anna's, shock and fury burn in his guts, pushing him to the edge of madness.

Garret has to force himself to recall Baylis' last words when he left his cook-shop a few nights ago. *Whatever you do, speed and silence, Garret. Speed and silence.*

In the corner of his vision, the three men close in, their rain-soaked smokes forgotten, their hands balled to fists in their trouser pockets, their cold gaze attached to the stranger.

Garret leaps, swings his arm with as much force as he can muster, and brings the mallet down on the man's skull.

Fat Annie

The creaking of tired floorboards lets her hands fly from the table into her pockets. 'Ma'am?' grumbles through the door.

'Come in, Butcher.'

He opens the door and steps through, pulling his cap down and kneading it in his large hands. 'It is done.'

'I'm well aware of this. No complications?'

'No. O'Hare killed him and put him on Nate's cart; the Worthing twins drove him to Lambeth and sunk him.'

'Does Baylis know about it?' she asks.

'Not sure…umm. Don't think so.' His cap is now compressed to the size of a small apple.

'What do you mean by "don't think so?" Does he know or does he not?'

'They'll never tell him, what with his past as a copper. Who the devil knows where he gets all that information from?'

'Hmm,' Fat Annie says, her eyes focussing on Butcher's nervous hands. 'If that's all, get back to work.'

She opens a journal and pretends to read it, while her ears are pricked to catch the slightest movement of her employee.

Butcher clears his throat. 'You got money for this. I played my part, so I want to be paid my part.'

'Take Rose,' she says without looking up.

He snorts. 'I could have her whenever she's late with the rent.' He steps forward and presses his knuckles on Fat Annie's table. 'I want half of the money you got for this.'

'You do not understand,' she says sweetly. 'You can take Rose. She's entirely yours. I don't want to see her face anymore.'

Butcher straightens up, not certain if he understands correctly. He sticks a finger into his right ear and wiggles, plops the finger out and asks, 'Mine?'

Fat Annie nods and waves him away.

Butcher has to pull himself to together so as not to stagger from her room.

Rose

She observes her face in the half-blind looking glass. Almost a stranger's face. She doesn't look like a woman of twenty-five. She looks like a forty-year-old whore. The cankers at the corner of her mouth don't worry her much anymore. She knows it's the French gout and she knows the arsenic does little to prevent this ghastly death. But she might have years until then, the disease might not disfigure her greatly, perhaps she will not even have to suffer. But who can predict the future?

'I know it's not much,' Butcher says. 'Only one room in Phoenix Street, the neighbours are noisy, the street is as dirty as this one, but…'

'I have syphilis, Butcher. This is why she wants me gone.'

He kneads his cap and says, 'I know.'

'So you want to live with an old wasp, knowing you can't fuck her without getting ill, knowing she won't earn much money on the streets, that she'll clutter your room, and is of little use. Why?' The last word shoots out of her mouth with much harshness.

Butcher tips his head; the cap is hiding in his large hands. 'Because,' he begins quietly, 'because I like your hands.'

'My what?'

'Your hands. They are gentle.'

'You are mistaken. My hands are weak. They only appear gentle.'

180

'You don't need to work on the streets. My money is good enough for both of us.'

'Butcher, I'm a whore. Women like me don't make decent wives. I don't cook well, I don't keep a clean house, and I'll certainly not have your children. What do you want with me?'

Butcher mutters something unintelligible, staring at his feet.

'What?' Rose asks.

'Just want your company. Don't want to go to bed alone anymore. Just want a nice woman. You're a nice woman.'

She swallows the jeers she'd almost thrown at him. Never in her life had she believed Butcher could be lonely.

'I have the French gout,' she says again, her voice a rasping whisper.

'I know. Won't touch you, not like that, anyway.'

She looks down at her hands, wondering what might be so special about them. 'When must I leave?'

'I think she wants you gone by tonight.'

'Are you not tired of working for her?'

'Hmm,' he says.

Perhaps this question was already too private, she thinks. She nods at him, and begins packing her things into a bag, wondering what strangeness the future has in store for her.

Dance

Music pours out through the warehouse's windows, mingling with chatter and giggles of people within. Anna hears Garret's laugh — a cannon shot over tin pipes and fiddles. Leaving the chilly autumn breeze behind, she steps through the door frame into a crowd of neighbours. Half a foot above them shows his head with hair the colour of flames sticking out in all directions. The thought of a lion brushes her mind. The mane, the coarse skin on his palms.

'Oy, Anna!' booms across the hall, through music, laughter, and conversations. She tries to not look at him for too long, tries to hide the smile that takes hostage of her face. One of her hands goes up and waves half-heartedly; she adds a timid nod, then busies herself with a hunt for ale.

'Want some of mine?' he says a few seconds later. *How did he part the crowd so fast?* she wonders. And why would that stupid heart of hers gives a lurch at a man's offer to take a sip of his lukewarm ale? She turns and looks up at him, his jug already right under her nose. The encouraging grin makes her reach out with both hands. She takes a large gulp and, for safety, another.

'Thank you,' she says and pushes the drink back into his hands. 'So. What about that conspiracy?'

He grabs the jug too hastily and almost spills his ale. 'What?'

182

'I'd always believed the Worthing twins could only make jokes day in day out, but now you three are conversing with such gravity, it looks as if their sister died.' She claps a hand over her mouth. 'I'm sorry. Did someone die?'

'What?' Garret squeaks, jumping as a woman pushes past and slaps him heartily on his hindquarters. He twists his neck, but she's already gone.

'Was I in the way?' he wonders aloud, his eyebrows pushed together, his face bright red.

Anna frowns at him, sees how glad he is about the quick change of topic, and wonders what makes him so nervous.

He clears his throat. 'You're safe now to enter Clark's Mews, if you want.'

Her gaze flicks to the Worthing brothers, who stare back at her and then down at their drinks.

She grabs Garret's arm, one part of her needing to steady herself, one part wanting to shake him. 'What did you, the Worthing brothers, Nate, and Butcher do to the knife-man?'

He opens his mouth and snaps it shut again. A moment later, he asks, 'Who told you?'

'No one,' she answers as not to cry out, *you all did*. 'I made a guess. Is he arrested?' *Probably not*, her mind whispers sarcastically.

She sees Garret's brain rattling, and then coming to a decision. He bends down, his face close to hers. 'I'll tell you my secrets when you tell me yours.'

'Are you blackmailing me?'

183

'No. I'd rather not tell you about this at all.'

She nods. 'I don't know if I can ever tell you about...myself.'

'That's one of the reasons I offered the bargain. I knew you wouldn't take it.'

There's a heaviness in his expression, one she didn't expect to ever find there. She tips her head in agreement, deciding that patience is needed to solve this riddle.

He clears his throat, takes another large gulp from his ale, and says, 'So. What about a dance with an Irish thief?'

In the pit of Anna's stomach, her misgivings begin to twitch harder. 'You have that enormous ale—' *as a dancing partner,* she was about to add, when Garret looks down at it and tips the entire contents down his throat. His Adam's apple bobs eagerly as all that ale flows from jug to stomach. Streams trickle down his chin, wetting his shirt. He sets the empty vessel in a windowsill and grins mischievously; child-like happiness mingling with nervousness shine in his face. Ale froth adorns his stubble. Anna's chest is about to burst. She lets out a bark of laughter, wipes his chin with her palm, and curtsies.

'Splendid!' says Garret, takes her hand, and whirls her to the centre of the hall, where the music is louder, the crowd denser, and chests, shoulders, and bottoms inevitably bump into each other. The wild Irish music vibrates in her limbs; bold dancers kick and punch, regardless of potential damages

184

caused. Garret shields Anna and takes all impacts without a twitch.

Two or three dances in, someone large must have shoved him, for he stumbles forward, steps onto her foot, and runs his shoulder against the side of her head.

They catch one another and push through the madly dancing crowd, outside, where air and space offer relief. Panting and laughing, they tumble through the frame of the warehouse's door.

He bends down to inspect her head for bruises, softly brushing her skin and hair. Then, with fresh courage fuelled by ale and the wild dance, he tips her chin towards him and kisses her abused temple.

'Garret, I…' She heaves a sigh and takes a step away from him. The tittering of her heart confuses her. The urge to lean into him shocks her. She knows where this will lead. The first step will make the next necessary. And the next. She can't take them.

'Hmm,' says Garret and runs his fingertips across her cheekbone. 'No kissing, then. But I'm thirsty and I know you like the tea I brew. Come.' He tugs her hand gently and she allows him to lead her away, along the street, up the crooked stairs, and into his room.

The door closes. Instantly, the space feels like air before a thunderstorm. Charged and heavy, tickling sweat from one's brow.

She watches him make tea, then takes the offered cup and empties it. She clears her throat.

'Garret, you have to know that I cannot be... That I cannot...' Why does her vocabulary fail her now? She kicks his worm-eaten cupboard.

'I know what you want from me, and I cannot give it to you.' There, wasn't too complicated after all. But now that she's said it, something about it doesn't ring true.

'What do I want from you, Anna?' he asks softly.

'Bed me.'

'Oy!' He doesn't know where to put his hands. In the trouser pockets they go, hiding until she would allow him to take a step forward.

'You know I am...*a widow*.' For the lack of a better word, she uses the lie.

His eyes darken.

'He was a brutal man.' Her voice is pleading.

'Do you believe I want to hurt you?'

She opens her mouth, snaps it shut and shrugs.

'Why are you afraid of me?'

'Because arousal can be a destructive force. One grows blind to the other's...limits.' Her shoulders are quivering. She tries hard to push the three men from her mind; one after the other, the knife, the cut, the laughter. And although she likes — or perhaps even loves? — Garret's company, the fact that his presence stirs up the worst of her memories makes her dread these moments of weakness.

186

Weakness. What a precise description, she thinks. She grows weak when he is around. But an odd sense of power is taking possession of her, too. Confused by such illogical and contradicting emotions, she shakes her head.

While she is silent, his hands sneak out of his pocket and now pick up hers. 'I know,' he whispers, hoping he does indeed understand what she was trying to say. All he can see is her anxiety and dark memories pressing her down.

'The problem is,' she begins, 'I wish you would hold me. But I don't want you to believe you could do with me whatever strikes your fancy.'

'You want me to hold you?' His voice is filled with doubt and wonder. He sees her struggle. 'But you are afraid I might hurt you.' He nods to himself, then shakes his head. 'Why would I ever do that?' His brain rattles visibly. 'What did he do to you?'

'I will not talk about it, Garret.'

They are standing close to one another. Every one of his words wants to pull her near, yet hers want to push him away. No one surrenders. Time stands still.

'Well. Then…I'll hold you now,' he announces, chin set and hands not quite certain how to proceed.

She looks up at him. Her feet surprise her by taking the first step forward.

To him, it feels as though he soars. To her, as though she's lost her balance, falling forward and relinquishing all her power and control. His arms engulf her, and his face pushes into her hair. She smells his sweat and the spilled ale on his shirt. Memories of the dance make her smile. Pictures of the woman slapping Garret's behind. Had he not realised what this gesture meant? She picks out other scenes from her memories. Women smiling at him, encouraging him to invite them for a dance or a chat. He had appeared oblivious to them all; he was talking to friends and only raised an eyebrow or two over those giggly females.

Anna grins into his shirt. Her tension runs down her spine, and down her thighs. She wiggles her toes to chase away the itch of fear and leans against his warm chest, wraps her arms around his torso, inhaling his aroma.

'Come,' he breathes into her hair, then lifts her up and carries her to his bed. Too late, he sees her face. 'I wasn't...' He stammers and sets her down onto her feet. 'I'm sorry. I know nothing about all this.' He makes a sweeping gesture with his arm, including her and the bed. 'I just thought that... I wished I could see your face, and   caress you and hold you. Somehow, it felt awkward doing that upright. Your neck will hurt when you have to look up all the time.'

She tries hard to hold back the snort. Pressing her face against his chest, a quiet huff escapes her lips.

His apparent naivety calms her nerves. She gazes at the small mattress and the large man, her mind analysing all available data: her one night with three violent men weighs against the unknown. One

188

could extrapolate previous experience in two ways: either the three men are an exemplification of all male of the species, or they are but one example of a species' broad range of behaviour patterns. The probability of the latter was high, considering that some women appeared to have married kind men. On the other hand, no matter how many respectful encounters she'd had with Garret, it could all turn violent once she let him take off all her clothes. And yet, hadn't he already seen her half-naked? The probability of him forcing her appears low, yet too incalculable. Her analytic mind is blurred with fear — a more than unacceptable state.

She comes to the conclusion that statistics won't help her now. Two individuals in one room; a breadth of unknown outcomes. Only one thing she knows for certain — the terror of one night long past has a grip on her she isn't willing to tolerate much longer. She makes a scientific decision: an experiment is in order. Running away would prove her spineless.

She tips her chin at Garret.

He sits down on the mattress and his hands feel like foreign objects to him. With puppy-eyes he gazes up at her, wondering how many times he would do or say the wrong thing. She steps forward and kneels on his bed. Neither of them know what to do next.

'Lie down?' she suggests after a moment, not wanting to be the first in this weak position.

He obeys and drapes his arm across the bed, offering it to her. Awkwardly, she nestles close to him, her head on his shoulder.

'Tell me about you,' she whispers and Garret begins his tale, all the while caressing her short curls, her cheeks, her eyebrows. Well past midnight, she falls asleep in his arms.

***

Anna's hand is still resting on his warm chest. The gentle up and down of his breath, his arm around her, and his fingers trailing through her hair spread a warm feeling in her stomach. Her eyes flutter open and meet Garret's.

Her cheeks blush. She stretches out her hand and begins to trace his lips with her fingertips, wondering how it might feel to kiss him. How it would feel to be kissed.

Garret waits, marvelling at her soft touch, her face, those dark eyes. He's hit by her determination when her nose touches his. She inhales his aroma and, not quite ready for his mouth just yet, kisses his brow.

A soft hiss escapes his nostrils. He tips his face towards her, eyes begging. She commands all her courage and lays her lips upon his, her mind blaring warnings, her legs ready to run should the need arise.

Garret, knowing nothing of her inner battle, slides his hands up her back and holds her face softly. Anxious not to make a wrong move, he is all ears, eyes, and fingertips. He sees her freeze, so he caresses away one fear, hoping the next won't follow too soon.

He watches her eyes, the tilt of her mouth, the softness of her hands when he opens the first button of her dress. She freezes again, her breath stumbles, so he retreats to her face and hair.

They dance together, one step forward, one back, two steps forward, one back. When he touches her bare breast and hides it in his large hand, Anna begins to shiver severely. She feels she stepped across a line, or somehow drifted over it, and there seems to be no return.

Shocked by her reaction, Garret lays his face to her bosom, his voice heating her skin. 'Forgive me,' he whispers, feeling like the brute he is.

Angry with herself, Anna buries her fingers in his hair and pulls him towards her. 'Kiss me,' she whispers, and he obeys.

Her hands tremble as she unbuttons his shirt. She knows she's standing in her own way. She slaps at her fears and takes a plunge, using his naivety as her safety net.

Garret — surprised and confused — takes her sudden decisiveness as arousal of some sort. He rids himself of all his clothes and presses his body to hers.

Anna's courage flies out the window.

He feels the rigidity of her body, sees the paleness in her face. Suddenly, he feels very inappropriately naked.

He sits up and moves a few inches away from her, covers her with the blanket and uses his pillow to hide his privates.

'Anna, I…I wish I could be close to you, but the closer I get, the more I scare you. And…I don't know how to do any of this right.

She tries to swallow, but her mouth and throat are too dry. 'You do nothing wrong,' she whispers and sits up, too. 'The only thing that scares me about you is that you are a man. You have a cock.'

Nonplussed, he looks at her. 'What do you want to do now?'

A master of simple questions, she diagnoses. 'I don't know what I want to do at this very moment. But I'm very certain that I don't want to go on being scared of you. Because that's what I am, and this realisation surprises me. I hadn't expected to still be afraid of men after all this time.' She bites her tongue, so as not to let the entire truth slip out. 'Would you show me how it is done properly?'

'Show what?'

She opens the last few buttons of her dress, pushes it over her shoulders and down to her waist.

Garret's brain clicks. 'I'm clumsy,' he stammers, suddenly too aware of his bulk.

'I am, too.'

He stares at his hands that always appear too crude to him when she's near. He's afraid he might hurt her with those paws of his. He tries to see himself with her eyes, but nothing special or appealing reveals itself.

Her slender hand sneaks into his strong one. 'You know,' she begins. 'Perhaps neither of us is clumsy. I'm really good at treating gunshot wounds, and you are the best burglar in the neighbourhood. I bet you can pick the most delicate locks.'

He chuckles and pokes her ribcage. After a while, he moves closer to her.

'Here?' he asks as he touches her neck.

'Yes,' she answers. 'Here?' she asks in return and lays her fingers onto his chest.

'Yes, please,' he hums as he lies down next to her, and they continue their dance; two forward, one back.

When he pulls her dress down her outstretched legs, she follows his moves with wide open eyes. His hands curl around her ankle and slide up into the hollow of her knee. She flinches when his fingers dip into the black curls atop her pubic bone.

'What are you doing?' she asks when he moves away from her.

'Kissing you.' His mouth is already covering her thighs. She quivers, nervous and a little amused about the mere thought of his lips touching her there.

A jolt arches her back when he takes a taste of her. Images scamper past her eyelids — those of a lion sending his coarse tongue across her most sensitive parts.

Her brain is rattling away, busy analysing her own reactions to his touches, scrutinising his moves and moans. Somehow, she is still waiting for a turning of the leaf, for him to lose his senses and force her. At least she's tried. She isn't a coward.

But slowly, gradually, with every small kiss and and every soft caress, her body demands more attention. The pulling and yearning someplace behind her navel, the heaviness of her sex, the quickening of her core. Her mind makes one last attempt at sharp observance and control. Then, Garret sighs softly, and her desire to taste his lips is too overwhelming. She grabs a fistful of his hair and pulls him towards her.

He follows her order, then stops, and traces a scar from her left hipbone to her right. 'What happened there? Was that him?'

'Yes.' Not quite a lie. *One* of them. 'I'm unable to bear children.'

His face falls into his hand, his breath staggers. 'If only we had met before this,' he whispers, placing his palm on the old injury. He covers her belly with kisses, then pushes himself up to her, caresses her face, whispering soothingly. Her throat constricts, her stomach aches, half with pain, half with longing.

'Garret,' she whispers in his ear as her hand moves from his chest down along his belly. 'Show me.' Tentatively, she touches him. It feels foreign; like a weapon on a man too gentle to know how to use it.

He guides her on top of him, kissing her lips, her cheeks and earlobes, her neck and shoulders. She lowers herself onto him until she feels his touch on her vulva. Her eyes close while she tests a little more pressure, and a little more yet.

He trembles beneath her, his breath ragged against her forehead. Slowly she slides down further, senses how he begins to enter this one part of her three men had befouled and torn apart years ago.

Garret feels his control slipping. He tightens his grip, makes a sound like a wounded animal, and calls her name. His hips tilt forwards in one forceful reflex.

His eyes snap open. He takes her face in his hands and makes her look at him. 'I am so sorry,' he says over and over again. 'I wasn't... I didn't mean to... I'm such an idiot!' He searches her face for pain, shock, or disgust, but finds only puzzlement. His arms wrap around her, protectively and consolingly, trying to undo any harm he might have caused.

Astounded at how precious she feels in his embrace and surprised that the burning in her sex doesn't reach her soul, a chuckle bursts from her chest. For her, one world had just collapsed and another was tearing wide open. She gazes at him, rakes her fingers through his orange mane, whispers, 'Clearly, we have to practice,' and continues her dance with the lion. Two steps forward, one back.

Sun

*L*ondon is covered in thick September morning fog. The windows of Garret's room seem to be made of dark-grey cotton, framed in white-washed wood. Anna blinks, rubs her eyes, and estimates the time to be five thirty or six o'clock. She catches herself wishing it would be a Sunday afternoon. The arm draped over hers and the warm body moulding itself against her back and legs make her want to remain where she is now.

Inch by inch, she turns around, hoping she doesn't wake him. He crinkles his lips and exhales a sigh. She takes in his unguarded expression, the pale-blue tinge of his eyelids and the movement underneath, and the stubble on his cheek that set her skin on fire. The mop of disorderly orange hair spread on the pillow makes her feel as though the sun has dropped into bed with her. Why had she ever thought him threatening?

She trails a finger over his shoulder, tries to span its width with one hand. The tip of a faint red line peeks through a gap between her fingers.

His wrist twitches as his hand wakes up. He strokes her back, and presses her to him before his eyes are fully open. 'Hmm...' he breathes when the church bell strikes six.

'I have to leave soon.'

He looks at her, his eyebrows drawn together, and brushes a black curl from her face. 'Are you alright? Wasn't I too...something?'

'You were certainly too something.' She grins at him, then grows serious. 'Lie on your stomach for a moment.'

He does as she asked, trying not to push her off the small mattress. 'It doesn't hurt, Anna. I already forgot it's there.'

Softly, she sends her fingers over the criss-crossing scars. 'After more than nine months in St Giles, observing disease, violence, and severe poverty, I still didn't learn to *not see*, nor will I ever learn to forget. This,' she lays a palm flat onto his back, 'will always hurt me, no matter how old the scars are. I'll never forget Poppy's face, either. Is she dead?'

Garret clears his throat. 'What did your husband do to you?'

She sighs and presses her face to his neck, wondering how many dark secrets can possibly stand between two lovers until the distance between them begins to grow.

He turns, wraps his arms around her, and kisses her face, her neck, and her bosom until she chuckles. 'When do you have to leave?'

'In half an hour.'

'Rather short, but...' he throws the blanket up and over both their heads. 'I need to see where exactly I have been too *something*. Them places might need soothing.'

'Such hasty medical treatment might be interpreted as sloppy and careless.'

'We can discuss it at length, or we can make an attempt at saving the patient.'

'Hard to tell which alternative would be the most reasonable,' she says. 'But I'd suggest an emergency treatment of all parts that had to endure your stubble.'

'Hmm. Can't remember all the places I put my mouth last night. Perhaps here?' he says and touches his lips to hers.

'All over, I'd wager.'

Helena

'William,' she whispers. 'Are you still not sleeping?' The boy cracks one eye open in response. 'It's late. Your mother won't be pleased.'

'But my head is so noisy, Miss Worthing, it wants me to stay awake.'

'What noises does it make?'

'Noises of the park we walked today, the pretty birdsong and children playing, and what Mother said about the countryside and Grandfather's house. And Father, who looked ill and upset. I always think of this. Did I upset him, Miss Worthing?'

She caresses his head and his warm cheek and says softly, 'Of course he is not upset with you, William. He has business to attend to and works hard. For you and your mother.'

'But he left and didn't return last night, and the night before. Did I make him leave?'

'Of course not. Shush now, you silly boy, and promise to not bother your mother with your strange thoughts. You'll only upset her.'

The boy squeezes both eyes shut, folds his hands under his chin, and whispers, 'I promise.'

'Good boy, William. Say your prayers.' She removes her hand from his hair, smoothes her dress, and leaves the nursery.

The boy is spoiled and overly sensitive, she thinks. How could his mother let this happen?

199

Surely, he was already like this when she arrived a year ago. A sickly child, too. Wouldn't survive a day without his mother pampering him. William this and William that.

Bristling with disapproval, she climbs the stairs to her room — a small compartment just beneath the attic where the servants live. She pushes the door into its frame. A soft creak, then silence. Her haven of privacy.

She undresses and washes with warm water the maid brought a few minutes earlier. She lies down flat on her bed, her legs straight out, her arms on her sides, face directed at the ceiling. A body methodically arranged, ready to drift off into bleak nothingness. But then, thoughts of her twin brothers creep through her skull.

Peter and Timothy. When she was a child, she spoke their names with love. Now she dreads the monthly meetings with them. She dreads their stories of hardship, their petty lives, their sour-smelling, thirdhand clothes, their fat wives and sick children, their ragged haircuts, their scrubby beards. Just thinking of their home makes her skin crawl. That hovel of a dwelling that reeks of shellfish gone bad and diapers gone rancid. It smells of something that will glue itself onto her, never let go, drag itself along when she returns to her well-kept room that smells of lemon juice the maid put into the water to wipe the windows and scrub the floors, threatening to turn all that she has accomplished with her own hard work into something just as rancid, stinky, diseased.

Whenever she meets her brothers, the word *discarded* scurries through her mind. Then, she quickly extracts all her savings — despite her resolutions not to — and gives Tim one pound and Pete another, knowing the money will melt away like the ice they use to keep their oysters fresh.

Surely she does wish to help, she tells herself then. It isn't bad conscience at all. Or, at least, not the only reason for her to regularly abandon all the savings she possesses.

And yet, every time she turns her back to her brothers to catch a cab back home, she feels as though she's bribed the rancid, stinky, and diseased thing to stay with them one month longer before it comes and feeds on her.

And so she returns to a warm and clean home, a respected occupation, to plenty of good food and pretty dresses, feeling guilty instead of grateful. *Shame on you! Say ten Ave Marias!*

It wasn't her brothers' fault, and had never been. When Father lost his shops and his houses, he took to drink so heavily that soon, the family found themselves without means.

Now she's glad for the piano and poetry lessons her father insisted on. Without them, she couldn't have obtained a position as governess. Her brothers, however, hadn't been able to obtain anything but a costermonger's cart to start a shellfish business in the slums. Selling shellfish no one else would eat but the wretched.

She blinks, absentmindedly fingering the letter she keeps under her pillow. The crinkled sheet of thin paper has been read so often, wept upon, and folded to a small rectangle again and again, that one can barely decipher the writing now. She knows its contents by heart. The whore was murdered. A gentleman did it. The tone her brothers had used allows only one conclusion.

She's afraid. Will God forgive her if she says nothing about it? *Thou shall not kill!* But wouldn't she kill them if she told the police and they were hung? Still, she dearly hopes they won't be caught. But then, doesn't that mean she wishes that man to be dead? How can there be redemption, if sin lies in every direction no matter which way she turns?

Condemned be the unlucky day when she and her brothers saw this girl with the cruelly cut-up face! Condemned shall she be herself for this one night, when she was at her lowest and had to seek refuge in Alf's attic. Perhaps the girl would still be alive had she never lodged there, never known it, or if she'd simply kept her mouth shut.

A soft knock interrupts her thoughts and pulls her from the past to the present.

When the dark shadow of her master approaches, she feels her cheeks glow like those of a child waiting for candy. She knows she mustn't give herself to a married man. But he needs her so. He cannot be without her, he said, before he lay with her the first night. And it surely didn't help her resolution that his hands were knowing and gentle, his manhood strong.

He lifts the corner of her blanket. 'How are you, my dear Helena?' he whispers.

202

***

He's barely able to keep his hackles down, so great the pleasure of triumph. He slides his tongue across his incisors and forces the grin off his face before he plants a kiss on the woman's lips.

Astonishing how incidents fall into perfect place and time, how a small bribe — merely pocket money — can redirect a mob in full rage. Whoever that man was who'd been killed, he doesn't feel sorry for him. This man will always shine like a beacon of his own glory. He imagines him floating down the river, a sack of clothes hugging a limp body, lazily drifting out onto the sea, waves lapping at it, fish nibbling. Or perhaps, his pockets had been filled with stones and his skin is already perforated and his flesh gnawed at by the countless bottom-dwelling fish and crayfish.

He pushes his hand underneath the woman's nightgown and her sighs make his already rock-hard erection ache with fury.

He growls. Low, and guttural. Wolf-like.

Such triumph! Despite his unforgivable mistake. But he'd never again allow himself such carelessness, such rage. But the brilliance of it! *His* brilliance!

He cares little that he must find a new territory now. A new playground. In fact, he's *thrilled*. So many slums in this city, countless whores.

Like this one.

203

She rocks her voluptuous hips against his narrow ones, and his mind and body answer with a scream for release.

Behind his eyes, images begin to fade — those of a body in the river, of the girl with an artfully carved grin, and the map on his desk, the streets' criss-crossing, the Thames' meandering.

His eager fingers dig into her large buttocks, and his hips lodge between her welcoming thighs. It doesn't take long.

Preview of the next book in the series:

𝔗𝔥𝔢 𝔇𝔢𝔳𝔦𝔩'𝔰 𝔊𝔯𝔦𝔫

History is indeed little more than the register of the crimes, follies, and misfortunes of mankind.

E. Gibbon

𝕴 finally found the peace to write down what must be revealed. At the age of twenty-seven, I witnessed a crime so outrageous that no one dared to tell the public. In fact, it has never been put in ink on paper — not by police, journalists, or historians. The general reflex was to forget what had happened.

I will hide these journals in my old school and beg the finder to make public what they contain. Not only must the crime be revealed, but I also wish to paint a different picture of a man who came to be known as the world's greatest detective.

Summer, 1889

𝕺ne of the first things I learned as an adult was that knowledge and fact meant nothing to people who were subjected to an adequate dose of fear and prejudice.

This simple-mindedness was the most disturbing attribute of my fellow two-legged creatures. Yet, according to Alfred Russel Wallace's

newest theories, I belonged to this same species —
the only one among the great apes that had
achieved bipedalism and an unusually large brain.
As there was no other upright, big-headed ape, I
must be human. But I had my doubts.

My place of work, the ward for infectious
diseases at Guy's Hospital in London, was a prime
example of the aforementioned human bias against
facts. Visitors showed delight when entering through
the elegant wrought-iron gate. Once on the hospital
grounds, they were favourably impressed by the
generous court with lawn, flowers, and bushes. The
white-framed windows spanning from floor to
ceiling of bright and well-ventilated wards gave the
illusion of a pleasant haven for the sick.

Yet, even the untrained eye should not have
failed to notice a dense overpopulation: each of the
forty cots in my ward was occupied by two or three
patients, bonded together by their bodily
fluids,oozing either from infected wounds or raw
orifices. Due to the chronic limitation of space,
doctors and nurses had learned to disregard what
they knew about transmission of disease under
crowded conditions: death spread like fire in a dry
pine forest.

However, everyone considered the situation
acceptable simply through habit. The slightest
change would have required the investment of
energy and consideration; neither willingly spent for
anyone but oneself. Therefore, nothing changed.

If I had an even more irascible temperament
than I already possessed, I would have openly held

hospital staff responsible for the deaths of countless patients who had lacked proper care and hygiene. But then, the ones who entrusted us with their health and well-being should share the guilt. It was common knowledge that the mortality of patients in hospitals was at least twice that of those who remained at home.

Sometimes I wondered how people could have possibly got the idea that medical doctors could help. Although circumstance occasionally permitted me to cure disease, this sunny Saturday held no such prospect.

The wire a nurse handed me complicated matters further: *To Dr Kronberg: Your assistance is required. Possible cholera case at Hampton Waterworks. Come at once. Inspector Gibson, Scotland Yard.*

***

I was a bacteriologist and epidemiologist, the best to be found in England. This fact could be attributed mostly to the lack of scientists working within this very young field of research. In all of London, we were but three — the other two had been my students. For the occasional cholera fatality or for any other victim who seemed to have been felled by an angry army of germs, I was invariably summoned.

As this call came with some frequency, I had the pleasure of working with Metropolitan Police inspectors once in a while. They were a well-mixed bunch of men whose mental sharpness ranged from that of a butter knife to an overripe plum.

Inspector Gibson belonged to the plum category. The butter knives, fifteen in total, had been assigned to the murder division — a restructuring effort within the Yard in response to the recent Whitechapel murders and the hunt for the culprit commonly known as Jack the Ripper.

I slipped the wire into my pocket and asked the nurse to summon a hansom. Then I made my way down to my basement laboratory and the hole in the wall that I could call my office. I threw a few belongings into my doctor's bag and rushed to the waiting cab.

***

The bumpy one-hour ride to Hampton Water Treatment Works was pleasant; it offered views London had long lost: greenery, fresh air, and once in a while, a glimpse of the river that still had the ability to reflect sunlight. Once the Thames entered the city, it turned into the dirtiest stretch of moving water in the whole of England. Crawling through London, it became saturated with cadavers from each of the many species populating the city, including their excrements. The river washed them out onto the sea, where they sank into the deep to be forgotten. London had an endless supply of filth, enough to defile the Thames for centuries to come. At times, this tired me so much that I felt compelled to pack my few belongings and move to a remote village. Perhaps to start a practice or breed sheep, or do both and be happy. Unfortunately, I was a scientist and my brain needed exercise. Country life would soon become dull, I was certain.

The hansom came to a halt at a wrought-iron gate with a prominent forged iron sign arching above it, its two sides connecting pillars of stone. Behind it stretched a massive brick complex adorned by three tall towers.

Hampton Water Treatment Works were built in response to the 1852 Water Act, after the progressive engineer Thomas Telford had annoyed the government for more than twenty years. He had argued that Londoners were drinking their own filth whenever they took water from the Thames, which resulted in recurring cholera outbreaks and other gruesome diseases. The inertness of official forces whenever money and consideration were to be invested amazed me rather often.

Roughly half a mile east from where I stood, an enormous reservoir was framed by crooked willows and a variety of tall grasses. My somewhat elevated position allowed me to look upon the water's dark blue surface decorated with hundreds of white splotches. The whooping, shrieking, and bustling about identified them as water birds.

I stepped away from the cab. Low humming seeped through the open doors of the pumping station; apparently, water was still being transported to London. A rather unsettling thought, considering the risk of cholera transmission.

I walked past three police officers — two blue-uniformed constables and one in plain clothes ,being Gibson. The bobbies answered my courteous nod with a smile, while Gibson looked puzzled.

The man I was aiming for was, I hoped, a waterworks employee. He was a bulky yet healthy-looking man of approximately seventy years of age. His face was framed by bushy white whiskers and mutton chops topped up with eyebrows of equal consistency. He gave the impression of someone who would retire only when already dead. And he was looking strained, as though his shoulders bore a heavy weight.

'I am Dr Anton Kronberg. Scotland Yard called me because of a potential cholera fatality in the waterworks. I assume you are the chief engineer?'

'Yes, I am. William Hathorne, pleased to make your acquaintance, Dr Kronberg. It was me who found the dead man.'

I noticed Gibson huffing irritably. Probably I undermined his authority yet again. Although it would require a certain degree of learning ability on his part, I was still surprised that he obviously hadn't yet become accustomed to my impertinence.

'Was it you who claimed the man to be a cholera victim?' I enquired.

'Yes.'

'But the pumps are still running.'

'Open cycle. Nothing is pumped to London at the moment,' Mr Hathorn supplied.

'How did you know he had cholera?'

He harrumphed, his gaze falling down to his shoes. 'I lived on Broad Street.'

'Oh. I'm sorry,' I said quietly, wondering whether the loss of his wife or even a child had burned the haggard and bluish look of a cholera death into his memory. Thirty-five years ago, the public pump on Broad Street had infected and killed more than six hundred people, marking the end of London's last cholera epidemic. People had dug their cesspit too close to the public pump. As soon as both pump and cesspit were shut down, the epidemic ceased.

With a tightening chest, I wondered how many people would have to die when a cholera victim floated in the drinking water supply of half the Londoners.

'Did you move the body, Mr Hathorne?'

'Well, I had to. I couldn't let him float in that trench, could I?'

'You used your hands, I presume.'

'What else would I use? My teeth?'

Naturally, Mr Hathorne looked puzzled. While explaining that I must disinfect his hands, I bent down and extracted the bottle of creosote and a large handkerchief from my bag. A little stunned, he let me proceed without protest.

'You kept your eyes open. I could see that when I came in. Can you tell me who else touched the man?'

With shoulders squared and moustache bristled, he replied, 'All the police officers, and that

211

other man over there.' His furry chin pointed towards the ditch.

Surprised, I turned around and spotted the man Hathorne had indicated. He was tall and unusually lean, and for a short moment I almost expected him to be bent by the wind and sway back and forth in synchrony with the high grass surrounding him. He was making his way up to the river and soon disappeared among the thick vegetation.

Gibson approached, hands in his trouser pockets, face balled to a fist. 'Dr Kronberg, finally!'

'I took a hansom; I can't fly,' I retorted and turned back to the engineer.

'Mr Hathorne, am I correct in assuming that the pumps — when not running in open cycle — take water from the reservoir and not directly from the trench?'

'Yes, that is correct.'

'So the contaminated trench water would be greatly diluted?'

'Of course. But who knows how long the dead fella was floating in there.'

'Is it possible to reverse the direction of the water flow and flush it from the trench back into the Thames?'

He considered my question, pulled his whiskers, then nodded.

'Can you exchange the entire volume three times?'

'I certainly can. But it would take the whole day...' He looked as though he hoped I would change my opinion.

'Then it will take the whole day,' I said. 'Thank you for your help, Mr Hathorne.' We shook hands, then I turned to Gibson. 'Inspector, I will examine the body now. If you please?'

Gibson squinted at me, tipped his head a fraction, then lead the way up the path.

'I will take a quick look at the man. If he is indeed a cholera victim, I need you to get me every man who touched his body.' After a moment of consideration, I added, 'Forget what I said. I want to disinfect the hands of every single man who entered the waterworks today.'

I knew Gibson didn't like to talk too much in my presence. He disliked me and my harsh replies. And I had issues with him, too. After having met him a few times, it was quite obvious that he was a liar. He pretended to be hard-working, intelligent, and dependable, while his constables backed him up constantly. Yet he was still an inspector at the Yard, and I was certain that being the son of someone important had put him there.

We followed a narrow path alongside the broad trench connecting the river to the reservoir. I wondered about its purpose — why store water when great quantities of it flowed past every day? Perhaps because moving water was turbid and the reservoir allowed the dirt to settle and the water to clear? I should have asked Hathorne about it.

Gibson and I walked through the tall grass; if I strayed off the path — and I felt compelled to do so — its tips would tickle my chin. Large dragonflies whizzed past me, one almost colliding with my forehead. They did not seem to be accustomed to human invasion. The chaotic concert of water birds carried over from the nearby reservoir. The nervous screeching of small sandpipers mingling with the trumpeting of swans and melancholic cries of a brace of cranes brought back memories of my life many years ago.

The pretty thoughts were wiped away instantly by a whiff of sickly sweet decomposition. The flies had noticed it, too, and all of us were approaching a small and discarded-looking pile of clothes containing a man's bluish face. A first glance told me that the corpse had spent a considerable time floating face down. Fish had already nibbled off the soft and protruding flesh — fingertips, lips, nose, and eyelids.

The wind turned a little, and the smell hit me directly now. It invaded my nostrils and plastered itself all over my body, clothes, and hair.

'Three police men are present. Why is that?' I asked Gibson. 'And who is the tall man who just darted off to the Thames? Is this a suspected crime?'

The inspector dropped his chin to reply as someone behind me cut across in a polite yet slightly bored tone, 'A dead man could not have climbed a fence, so Inspector Gibson here made the brilliant conclusion that someone must have shoved the body into the waterworks.'

214

Surprised, I turned around and had to crane my neck to face the man who had spoken. He was a head taller than I and wore a sharp and determined expression. He seemed to consider himself superior, judging from the snide remark about Gibson and the amount of self-confidence he exuded that bordered on arrogance. His attire and demeanour spoke of a man who had most likely enjoyed a spoiled upper-class childhood.

Keen, light grey eyes pierced mine for a moment, but his curiosity faded quickly. Apparently, nothing of interest had presented itself. I was greatly relieved. For a moment, I had feared he would see through my disguise. But as usual, I was surrounded by blindness.

The sharp contrast between the two men in front of me was almost ridiculous. Gibson was lacking facial muscles and possessed a lower lip that seemed to serve more the purpose of a rain gutter than a communication tool. Almost constantly, he worked his jaws, picked and chewed his nails, and perspired on the very top of his skull.

'Mr Holmes, this is Dr Anton Kronberg, epidemiologist from Guy's,' said Gibson. I reached out my hand, which was taken, squeezed firmly, and quickly dropped as though it was infected. 'Dr Kronberg, this is Mr Sherlock Holmes,' finished the inspector, making it sound as though I should know who Sherlock Holmes was.

'Has the victim been pushed into the trench, Mr Holmes?' Gibson enquired.

'Unlikely,' Mr Holmes answered.

'How can you tell?' I asked.

'There are no marks on either side of the Thames's water edge, the body shows no signs of being transported with a hook, rope, a boat, or similar, and…'

The man trailed off and I made a mental note to go and check the Thames's flow to ascertain that a body could indeed float into the trench without help.

Mr Holmes had begun staring at me with narrowed eyes. His gaze flew from my slender hands to my small feet, swept over my slim figure and my not-very-masculine face. Then his attention got stuck on my flat chest for a second. A last look to my throat, the nonexistent Adam's apple hidden by a high collar and cravat, and his eyes lit up in surprise. A slight smile flickered across his face while his head produced an almost imperceptible nod.

Suddenly, my clothes felt too small, my hands too clammy, my neck too tense, and the rest of my body too hot. I was itching all over and forced myself to keep breathing. The man had discovered my best-kept secret within minutes, while others had been fooled for years. I was standing among a bunch of policemen and my fate seemed sealed. I would lose my occupation, my degree, and my residency to spend a few years in jail. When finally released, I would do what? Embroider doilies?

Pushing past the two men, I made for the Thames to get away before doing something reckless and stupid. I would have to deal with Holmes when he was alone. The notion of throwing him into the river appeared very attractive, but I flicked the silly thought away and forced myself to focus on the business at hand.

First I needed to know how the body could have possibly got into that trench. The grass was intact; no blades were bent except for where I had seen Mr Holmes walk along. I looked around on the ground, Mr Holmes observing my movements.

Only one set of footprints was visible, which must have been Mr Holmes's. I picked up a few rotten branches and dry twigs, broke them into pieces of roughly arm's length, and cast them into the Thames. Most of them made it into the trench and drifted towards me. A sand bank was producing vortexes just at the mouth, causing my floats to enter the trench instead of being carried away by the much greater force of the river. The chance was high that it was only the water that had pushed the body in here.

'It seems you were correct, Mr Holmes,' I noted while passing him. He didn't appear bored anymore. When I walked back to the corpse, my stomach felt as if I had eaten a brick.

I extracted a pair of India rubber gloves from my bag and put them on. Mr Holmes squatted down next to me, too close to the corpse for my taste.

'Don't touch it, please,' I cautioned.

He didn't hear me, or else simply ignored my remark; his gaze was already sweeping over the dead man.

The exposed face and hands of the corpse told me he had been in the water for approximately thirty-six hours.

Thinking that attack is always better than premature retreat, I turned to Mr Holmes. 'Do you happen to know how fast the Thames flows here?'

He did not even look up, only muttered, 'Thirty miles from here at the most.'

'Considering which duration of exposure?'

'Twenty-four to thirty-six hours.'

'Interesting.' I was surprised at his apparent medical background; he had correctly assessed the time the man had spent in the water. He had also calculated the maximum distance the corpse could have travelled downstream.

I cast a sideways glance at the man and got the impression that he vibrated with intellectual energy wanting to be utilised.

'You are an odd version of a private detective. One the police call in? I never heard of their doing so before,' I wondered aloud.

'I prefer the term *consulting detective*.'

'Ah…' I replied absent-mindedly while my attention was pulled back to the body. He was extremely emaciated; the skin with the typical blue tinge looked paper thin — most definitely cholera in the final stage. I was about to examine his clothes for signs of violence when Mr Holmes barked, 'Stop!'

Before I could protest, he pushed me aside, pulled a magnifying glass from his waistcoat pocket, and hovered over the corpse. The fact that his nose almost touched the man's coat was rather unsettling.

'What is it?'

'He has been dressed by someone else,' he noted.

'Show me!'

Looking a little irritated, he handed me his magnifying glass and I took it after pulling my gloves off. The thick rubber hindered my work and made me feel like a butcher. I could disinfect my hands later.

Mr Holmes started to talk rather fast then. 'The man was obviously right-handed — that hand having more calluses on the palms. Yet you will observe greasy thumbprints pushing in from the left-hand side of his coat buttons.'

I spotted the prints, put my nose as close as possible, and sniffed — corpse smell, Thames water, and possibly the faintest hint of petroleum.

'I smell petroleum; perhaps from an oil lamp,' I remarked quietly.

Upon examining his hands, I found superficial scratches, swelling and bruises on the knuckles of the right hand. Probably from a fist fight only a day or two before his death — odd, given his weakness. His hands seemed to have been strong and rough once, but he had not been doing hard work with them for a while now, for the calluses had started to peel off. His fingernails had multiple discolourations, showing that he had been undernourished and sick for weeks before contracting cholera. He must have been very poor during his last few months, and I

219

wondered where he had come from. His clothes looked worn and too big now, and a lot of debris from the river had collected in them. I examined his sleeves, turned his hands around, and found a pale red banding pattern around his wrists.

'Restraint marks,' said Mr Holmes. 'The man used to be a farm worker but lost his occupation three to four months ago.'

'Could be correct,' I answered. He had obviously based his judgement on the man's clothes, boots, and hands.

'But the man could have had any other physically demanding occupation, Mr Holmes. He could as well have been a coal mine worker. The clothes are not necessarily his.'

Mr Holmes sat erect, pulling one eyebrow up. 'We can safely assume that he had owned these boots for about ten years,' said he while extracting a bare foot and holding its shoe next to it. The sole, worn down to a thin layer of rubber, contained a major hole where the man's heel used to be and showed a perfect imprint of the shape of the man's foot and toes.

'I figured that you must have taken a closer look at him before I arrived, for you spoke about the lack of signs of transport by a boat, a hook, or rope. Now it appears you've touched and even undressed the corpse?'

'Unfortunately it was but a superficial examination, for I found it more pressing to investigate how he had entered the trench.'

I nodded, not at all relieved. 'Mr Holmes, you have put your hands to your face at least twice, even scratched your chin very close to your lips. That is rather reckless considering that you have touched a cholera victim.'

Now the other eyebrow went up, too. I passed him a handkerchief soaked in creosote and he wiped himself off with care. Then, without touching the corpse, he bent down low over it and pointed. 'What is this?' The genuine interest in his voice was bare of indignation, as if he had not taken offence. I was surprised and wondered whether he did not mind being corrected by a woman or whether he was so focused on the examination that he had no time to spend on feeling resentful.

I picked at the smudge he had indicated. It was a small green feather that was tucked into a small tear just underneath the coat's topmost buttonhole. I smoothed it and rubbed off the muck.

'An oriole female. How unusual! I haven't heard their call for many years.'

'A rare bird?' asked Mr Holmes.

'Yes, but I can't tell where this feather would have come from. I have never heard the bird's call in the London area. The man may have found the feather anywhere and could have been carrying it around for quite a while…' I trailed off, gazing at the small quill and the light grey down.

'The quill is still somewhat soft,' I murmured, 'and the down is not worn. This feather wasn't plucked by a bird of prey or a fox or the like; it was moulted. He had it for a few weeks at the most, that means he must have found it just before he became ill, or someone gave it to him while he was sick.'

Mr Holmes looked surprised, and I felt the need to explain myself. 'In my childhood I spent rather too much time in treetops and learned a lot about birds. The quill tip shows that the feather has been pushed out by a newly emerging one; birds start moulting in spring. The farther north they live, the later they start. The bird shed this feather in late spring or midsummer this year. Wherever this man had spent his last days is close to a nesting place of an oriole pair. A female is never alone at this time of year.'

'Where do these birds live?' he enquired.

'Large and old forests with dense foliage and water, such as a lake or a stream. An adjacent wetland would do, too.'

'The Thames?'

'Possibly,' I mused.

The brick in my stomach had become unbearable. 'Mr Holmes, are you planning to give me away?'

He looked surprised, then waved his hand at me. 'Pshaw!' he exclaimed, almost amused now. 'Although I gather it is quite a complicated issue. You don't fancy going to India, I presume.' The latter wasn't so much a question as a statement.

'Obviously I don't.'

He probably did not know that obtaining a medical degree in Germany was still forbidden for women. If my true identity were revealed, I would lose my occupation and my British residency, be deported, and end up in a German jail. My alternative, although I did not consider it one, would be to go to India. The few British women who had recently managed to get a medical degree had eventually given in to the mounting social pressure and left for India, out of the way of the exclusively male medical establishment. To the best of my knowledge, I was the only exception.

'I had hoped it would not be as evident,' I said quietly.

'It is evident only to me. I fancy myself as rather observant.'

'So I've noticed. Yet you are still here, despite the fact that this case appears to bore you. I wonder why that is.'

'I haven't formed an opinion yet. But it does indeed seem to be a rather dull case. I wonder...' Thoughtfully, he gazed at me and I realised that he had stayed to analyse me — I represented a curiosity.

'What made you change your identity?' he enquired as his face lit up with interest.

'That's none of your business, Mr Holmes.'

Suddenly, his expression changed as his *modus operandi* switched to analysis, and, after a minute, he seemed to have reached a conclusion. 'I dare say that guilt was the culprit.'

'What?'

'As women weren't allowed a higher education a few years ago, you had to cut your hair and disguise yourself as a man to be able to study medicine. But the intriguing question remains: *Why* did you accept such drastic measures for a degree? Your accent is evident; you are a German who has learned English in the Boston area. Harvard Medical School?'

I nodded; my odd mix of American and British English and the German linguistic baggage were rather obvious.

'At first I thought you lived in the East End, but I was wrong. You live in or very near St Giles.' He pointed a long finger to the splashes on my shoes and trousers. I wiped them every day before entering Guy's, but some bits always remained.

'The brown stains on your right index finger and thumb appear to be from harvesting parts of a medical plant. The milk thistle, I presume?'

I cleared my throat; this was getting too far for my taste. 'Correct,' I said, preparing for battle.

'You treat the poor free of charge, considering the herb, which certainly is not used in hospitals. And there is the location in which you choose to live — London's worst rookery! You seem to have a tendency towards exaggerated philanthropy!' He tipped an eyebrow, his mouth lightly compressed. I could see a mix of amusement and dismissal in his face.

'You don't care much about the appearance of your clothes,' he went on, ignoring my cold stare. 'They are a bit tattered on the sleeves and the collar, but surely not for lack of money. You have too little time! You probably have no tailor blind enough to not discover the details of your anatomy.'

224

Here I shot a nervous glance over his shoulder, assessing the distance to Gibson or any of his men. Mr Holmes waved at me impatiently, as though my anxiety to be discovered by yet another man meant nothing to him.

He continued without pause. 'You have no one you could trust at your home, no housekeeper or maid who could keep your secret. That forces you to do everything for yourself. In addition will be your nightly excursions into the slums to treat your neighbours. You probably don't fancy sleep very much?' His voice was taunting now.

'I sleep four hours on average.' I wondered whether he had noticed that I analysed him, too.

He continued in a dry, machine-like *rat-tat-tat*. 'You are very compassionate, even with the dead.' He pointed to the corpse between us. 'One of the few, typical female attitudes you exhibit; although in your case it's not merely learned — there is weight behind it. I must conclude that you have felt guilty because someone you loved died. And now you want to help prevent that from happening to others. But you must fail, because death and disease are natural. Considering your peculiar circumstances and your unconventional behaviour, I propose that you come from a poor home. Your father raised you after your mother died? Perhaps soon after your birth? Obviously, there hasn't been much female influence in your upbringing.'

Utterly taken aback by the triumph in his demeanour, I snarled, 'You are oversimplifying, Mr Holmes.' Rarely had anyone made me that angry, and only with effort could I keep my voice under control. 'It's not guilt that drives me. I would not have got so far if not for the passion I feel for medicine. My mother did die and I resent you for the pride you feel in deducing private details of my life. Details I do not wish to discuss with you!'

The man's gaze flickered a little. 'I met people like you at Harvard, Mr Holmes. Brilliant men who need the constant stimulation of the brain and who see little else than their work. Your brain is running in circles when not put to hard work, and boredom is your greatest torture.'

Mr Holmes was rooted to the spot, his eyes unfocused, and behind them, his mind was racing.

'I have seen these men using cocaine when nothing is at hand to tickle their intellectual powers. What about you, Mr Holmes?' His gaze sharp now, his eyes met mine. I nodded and smiled. 'It doesn't help much, does it? Is it the cello that can put some order into that occasionally too-chaotic brain of yours?'

I pointed to his left hand.

'No,' I decided aloud, 'for the cello wants to be embraced. You prefer the violin — she can be held at a distance.'

He gazed at the faint calluses on the fingertips of his left hand, marks produced by pressing down strings.

'You are a passionate man and you can hide that well. But do you really believe that outsmarting everyone around you is an accomplishment?'

His expression was controlled and neutral, but his pupils were dilated to the maximum, betraying his shock.

I rose to my feet, took a step forward, and put my face close to his. 'It feels as though a stranger ripped off all your clothes, doesn't it?' I said softly. 'Don't you dare dig into my brain or private life again.' I tipped my hat, turned away, and left him in the grass.

Find **The Devil's Grin** and free extras on my webpage: anneliewendeberg.com

Acknowledgements

The murders in Whitechapel inspired some parts of this story, most of all Mr Steward, whose real name we'll, of course, never know. Many thanks to Stephen P. Ryder from *The Casebook*, as well as all contributors to the largest Jack the Ripper online resource.

I owe several characters to John Thomson and Adolphe Smith, who photographed and interviewed the people populating London's streets in the 1870s.

Scotty the Crawler and her friend (whom I named Betty in this book) lived and perished in St Giles under extreme poverty.

Baylis, a former policeman, did indeed own the cook-shop at Drury Lane, which was open to convicts and street arabs alike, and everyone else too poor to afford a meal, such as Ramo Sammy, who also appears in this book.

The hardships these people had to endure, and the compassion they practised, inspired me to try to bring them back to life.

Excerpts from *Street Life in London*, by John Thomson and Adolphe Smith (1876 to 1877, public domain):

'...among the poor he met with that charity which the poor more than any other class extend one towards the other.'

The Crawlers

Huddled together on the workhouse steps in Short's Gardens those wrecks of humanity, the Crawlers of St. Giles's, may be seen both day and night seeking mutual warmth and mutual consolation in their extreme misery. As a rule, they are old women reduced by vice and poverty to that degree of wretchedness which destroys even the energy to beg. They have not the strength to struggle for bread, and prefer starvation to the activity which an ordinary mendicant must display. As a natural consequence, they cannot obtain money for a lodging or for food. What little charity they receive is more frequently derived from the lowest orders. They beg from beggars, and the energetic, prosperous mendicant is in his turn called upon to give to those who are his inferiors in the "profession." Stale bread, half-used tea-leaves, and on gala days, the fly-blown bone of a joint, are their principal items of diet. A broken jug, or a tea-pot without spout or handle, constitutes the domestic crockery. In this the stale tea-leaves, or, perhaps, if one of the company has succeeded in begging a penny, a halfpenny-worth of new tea is carefully placed; then one of the women rises and crawls slowly towards Drury Lane, where there is a coffee-shop keeper and also a publican who take compassion on these women, and supply them gratuitously with boiling water.

A Convicts' Home

For fourteen years he (Baylis) has taken delight in serving the wretched people around him; but, remembering his own past experience, his generosity is unbounded towards the pale-faced street arabs who with hungry eyes frequently throng about his door. His thoughts are constantly occupied with the fate of these children, and he anxiously inquired whether I had any

229

hope that legislature would or could adopt some effective means of protecting the children who had no parents and are left to learn every vice in the streets of London. In the meanwhile, they can, in any case, obtain enormous helps of pudding for a penny, and even for a halfpenny. Nothing is wasted in this establishment. All scraps are used, and those who cannot afford to pay for a fair cut from the joint can obtain, for a penny or twopence, a collection of vegetables and scraps mixed with soup or gravy, that contain a good proportion of the nutritive properties of meat.

What began as a short story — initiated by Rita Singer's *I want more of that Irish hottie* comment on Facebook — developed into a novel over the past two years.

While I'm not quite certain how precisely this story came about (I wasn't really present, all I did was to scribble a bit), a supportive and trustworthy group of people helped me write it and push it towards publication: Magnus Wendeberg, who always has to read the awful first drafts; Rita Singer, who provides the most hilarious comments; Sabrina Flynn, who is my invaluable manuscript-over-the-head-slapper (and yes girl, I do have those imaginary conversations with you, too!); Nancy DeMarco, who patiently points out strengths and weaknesses of my texts since I first tried my hand on writing; Bryan Kroeger, whose warm and enthusiastic feedback is balm on a writer's soul; and

Heike Schmidt, who always asks for more (from Kronberg books to strawberry ice cream) Thank you all for your help and your patience with my unfinished stories! I hope you like the final outcome.

I'd also like to thank the National Library of Scotland for their wonderfully detailed maps of the 1890s London.

And the last bow goes to my proofreader, Susan Uttendorfsky, for helping me to not sound too non-native-y (Yes, I know this isn't even a word).

Made in the USA
Lexington, KY
14 April 2016